CLASSIC
ADVENTURES

This book belongs to

Name . . . .

Date . . . .

The Swiss Family Robinson

By
J. D. Wyss

The Classic Adventures Series

First published by Adam & Charles Black
This facsimile edition
© Fabbri Publishing Ltd 1992
Printed and bound in Spain by Printer
Industria Gráfica, Barcelona

ISBN 1-85587-335-4

CONTENTS

CHAPTER I

SHIPWRECK

... ALREADY the storm had continued six days; on the seventh its fury seemed still increasing; and the morning dawned upon us without a prospect of hope, for no one on board even knew where we were. My four boys clung to me in their fright, while my wife wiped the tears from her cheeks.

At this moment a cry of 'Land, land!' was heard through the roaring of the waves, and instantly the vessel struck against a rock so violently as to drive every one from his place; a tremendous cracking succeeded, as if the ship was going to pieces.

I hurried on deck, and saw a terrible sight. The crew had crowded into the boats till there was no room for us, and even as I appeared they cut the ropes to move off. I cried to them frantically not to leave us, but in vain, for the roaring of the sea prevented my being heard.

As all hope from this direction was over, I examined the ship to see if she would hold together for a little while, and was reassured. She was wedged stern first between two rocks, and it did not seem likely that the waves would drive her off at present. Therefore, when I returned to the cabin, which happened, fortunately, to be in the high part, and out of reach of the water, I was able to speak cheerfully of our position.

Comforted by this, my wife prepared something to eat, and the four boys at least ate heartily, and then the three youngest went to bed, and, tired out, soon were sleeping soundly. Fritz, the eldest, sat up with us.

'I have been thinking,' he said, 'that if we had some bladders or cork-jackets for mother and the others, you and I, father, could perhaps swim to land.'

I thought there was some sense in what he said, so, in case the ship should break up in the night, he and I looked about for some small empty barrels; these we tied two and two together, and fastened them under the arms of each child.

Fritz then lay down, and was soon asleep; but his mother and I kept watch throughout this awful night. In the morning the sky was brighter, and the wind had fallen.

The boys sprang up in capital spirits, and Fritz advised that we should swim to land while the sea was calm. Ernest, the second boy, protested, not being able to swim himself, and suggested a raft.

I sent them all to look about the ship, and bring what things they could find that were likely to be useful, while I and my wife discussed the situation.

Presently they all rejoined me, bringing various treasures. Fritz had two guns, some powder and shot and bullets; Ernest produced a lot of carpenter's tools; while Jack, the third boy, came up laughing on the back of a huge dog, named Turk, and followed by another called Flora. The poor creatures had almost knocked him down in their eagerness when he had released them; and though at first I thought more of the food they would eat than of their usefulness, I agreed they might certainly assist us in hunting should we ever get on shore.

Little Francis had found some fishing-hooks, at which his brothers mocked, until I reminded them it was likely we might have to depend for our food on fishing for some time to come.

My wife had found on board a cow and an ass, two goats, six sheep and a sow, which she had fed. All this was good so far as it went.

But now once more occurred to us the difficulty of crossing the broad strip of water that separated us from some kind of land, which we could just see far off. Jack, who was generally ready with an idea, cried out that he had often careered about on a pond at home in a tub, and that, as there seemed plenty of large barrels here, we might each have one and try.

This was not quite so simple as it sounded, but after some thinking I set to work, and, with the help of the boys, sawed four of the great barrels in half. This was tiring work, and took a long time, and there was much else to do before we could venture to trust ourselves on the water in them.

To make them more secure, we found a long pliant plank, and placed the eight tubs upon it, leaving a piece at each end reaching beyond the tubs. This being bent upward, like the keel of a vessel, made the whole contrivance more like a boat. We next nailed all the tubs to the plank, and afterwards put two other planks, of the same length as the first, on each side of the tubs. When all this was finished, we found we had produced a kind of narrow boat, divided into eight compartments. But then the difficulty was to move this great boat at all, for its weight was enormous. However, by putting rollers under it and using all our strength, we launched it into the sea. I had taken the precaution to attach a rope to it first, so it rode tethered; but, alas! in the first moment, we saw that it leaned far over to one side in a most alarming fashion. It soon occurred to me that this was only because it was so buoyant it danced up too far above the water, and after throwing some heavy things into the tubs, we saw it sink a little, and then float quite level.

However, all this had taken the whole day, and we had worked so hard that we had only eaten a bit of bread and taken a drink of milk occasionally, so now we sat down to a regular supper, and then went to bed, in high expectation of getting to the land next morning.

CHAPTER II

LANDING ON THE DESERT ISLAND

BY break of day we were all awake and alert, and I began to give orders to my little crew. First we gave each animal on board a hearty meal, and then put food and water enough for several days near them, as we hoped to come back and fetch them shortly. Our first cargo consisted of a barrel of gunpowder, three guns, and three rifles with ammunition, two pairs of pocket-pistols, a chest containing cakes of portable soup, another full of hard biscuits, an iron pot, a fishing-rod, a chest of nails and another of carpenter's tools, and, lastly, some sailcloth to make a tent.

When all was ready we each stepped bravely into a tub. At the moment of our departure the cocks and hens, of which there were numbers on board, began to cluck as if to protest against being left behind. So we put some of them into one of the tubs and covered it with planks, and left the rest of the fowls to themselves in the hope that they would follow us, the geese and the ducks by water, and the pigeons in the air.

We were waiting for my wife, who joined us loaded with a large bag, which she threw into the tub that already contained little Francis. I imagined that she intended it for him to sit upon, so asked no questions.

In the first tub, at the boat's head, was my wife.

In the second was little Francis, a boy of six years old, remarkable for his sweet disposition.

In the third, Fritz, the eldest, nearly sixteen, a handsome lad, full of intelligence and vivacity.

3

In the fourth was the barrel of gunpowder, with the cocks and hens and the sail-cloth.

In the fifth, the provisions of every kind.

In the sixth, Jack, my third son, a light-hearted, bold, careless boy, about thirteen years old.

In the seventh, Ernest, the second in age, a boy of fourteen, of a studious disposition, well read and thoughtful, but inclined to be both lazy and greedy.

In the eighth was I myself, holding a pole by which I steered, while I, as well as the others, was provided with an oar to propel the boat. The boys devoured with their eyes the blue land they saw at a distance. We rowed with all our strength to reach it, but at first the boat only turned round and round; at length I managed to steer so that it went in a straight line. As we started, the two dogs, after whining and running up and down the deck for a while, plunged into the sea and swam after us. They were too large for us to think of taking them in; but they did not try to climb up the sides of the boat, only rested their paws on the edges of the planks when they were tired.

Thus we proceeded slowly; but the nearer we approached the land, the more gloomy and unpromising it appeared. The coast was nothing but barren rocks. However, the sea was calm, and we could see casks, bales, chests, and other vestiges of the shipwreck, floating round us. We managed to get hold of two of these, and towed them after us in the water. As we drew nearer to the land, Fritz, who had keen eyes, saw some trees, and exclaimed that they were palm-trees. Ernest expressed his joy that he should now get much larger and better coconuts than those of Europe. Jack drew a small telescope from his pocket and handed it to me, so that by its aid I got a good idea of the shore, and saw a little opening between the rocks, near the mouth of a creek, towards which all our geese and ducks were heading. I steered for it too, and found it was the entrance to a little bay; the water was neither too deep nor too shallow to receive our boat. So we entered it and ran ashore.

The moment our unwieldy boat grated on the shingle the elder boys leaped out, and even little Francis, who had been wedged in his tub like a potted herring, sprang forward. The dogs, who had arrived first, greeted us with every demonstration of joy; the geese kept up a loud cackling, and the ducks contributed a deep quacking; the cocks and hens clucked; and the boys chattered all together. To this was added the disagreeable scream of some penguins and flamingoes,

4

which flew over our heads or sat on the points of the rocks at the entrance of the bay.

The first thing we did on finding ourselves safe on dry land was to fall on our knees and utter a short thanksgiving to God our Father.

We next unloaded the boat, and then looked about for a convenient place to set up a tent under the shade of the rocks. Having agreed upon a place, we set to work, and drove one of our poles firmly into a fissure of the rock; this rested upon another pole, which was driven perpendicularly into the ground. Over the ridge we threw some sail-cloth, and fastened it down on each side to the ground with stakes. The next thing to be done was to collect grass and moss, to be spread and dried in the sun, to serve us for beds. While the boys were doing this, I made near the tent a kind of little kitchen.

A few flat stones served for a hearth, and with some little twigs a brisk, cheering fire was soon alight. We put some of the soup-cakes, with water, into our iron pot over the flame. When Francis saw the soup-cakes he mistook them for glue, and asked with such an appearance of earnestness what we were going to stick together that his mother smiled as she explained that these cakes were made of the juices of meat, pressed out and consolidated to make them easy to pack.

In the meanwhile Fritz, taking one of the guns, had wandered along the side of the river; Ernest had gone to the seashore; and Jack took the direction of a chain of rocks which jutted out into the sea.

Presently I heard loud cries coming from Jack, and, snatching up my hatchet, I ran to his help. He was up to his knees in water, with a large sea lobster hanging on to his leg by its claws. I jumped into the water with such a splash that the creature let go his hold; but I caught him and carried him off, followed by Jack, who, having observed how I held the lobster by the back, laid his own hand upon it in the same way; but scarcely had he grasped it than he received a violent blow on the face from the lobster's tail, which made him drop the animal on the ground. In his rage he snatched up a stone, and killed it with a single blow. Then, fearless of a dead enemy, he carried it off triumphantly, crying:

'Mother, mother, a sea lobster! Ernest, a sea lobster! Where is Fritz? Take care, Francis; he will bite you.'

In a moment all were round him, examining the wonderful creature, and exclaiming at his enormous size.

'Yes, yes,' said Jack, holding up one of the claws; 'you may well wonder at his size. This was the frightful claw which seized my leg, but I have taught him what it is to attack *me*; I have paid him well.'

'Oh, oh, Mr. Boaster!' cried I, 'you give a pretty account of the matter. Now *mine* would be that, if I had not been near, the lobster would have shown you another sort of game. Believe me Jack, you have no great reason to boast of the adventure.'

Ernest suggested that the lobster had better be put into the soup; but this his mother opposed, observing that we must be more economical of our provisions than that, for the lobster of itself would furnish a dinner for the whole family.

I complimented Jack on his being the first to find an animal that might serve for food, and promised him, for his own share, the famous claw which had nipped him so tightly.

'Ah! but I have seen something too that is good to eat,' said Ernest; 'and I should have got it if it had not been in the water, so that I must have wetted my feet—'

'Oh, that is a famous story!' cried Jack. 'I can tell you what he saw — some nasty mussels. Why, I would not eat one of them for the world. Think of my lobster!'

'That is not true, Jack, for they were oysters, and not mussels, that I saw. I am sure of it, for they stuck to the rock.'

'Well,' said I, addressing Ernest, 'go and fetch some at once; you will have to get used to wetting your feet here, so the sooner you begin the better.'

'All right,' he answered: 'and at the same time I will bring home some salt which I saw in the holes of the rocks, where, I suppose, it had been left when the sea-water evaporated.'

'If you had brought some back at first instead of talking so much you would have done better,' said I.

When he returned, however, we found that he had still feared to get the oysters, and had scraped up so much sand with the salt that it appeared to be useless until my wife dissolved it in water, and then strained it through a piece of muslin, which left the sand and grit behind, so that we could season our soup with the salt water.

Then, when the soup was ready, we suddenly looked at each other and laughed, for we had quite forgotten to bring any sort of plates or spoons away from the wreck, and it would be impossible for each of us to raise the large boiling pot to his lips. It was a little like the fox in the fable, when the stork desires him to help himself from a vessel with a long neck. Ernest remarked that if we could but get some of the nice coconuts he often thought about, we might empty them and use the pieces of the shells for spoons.

'Yes, yes,' replied I, '*if we could but get some*. If wishing were any good, we might as well wish at once for a dozen silver spoons.'

'But at least,' said the boy, 'we can use some oyster-shells for spoons.'

'Good!' I said. 'Run quickly and fetch some of them.'

Jack ran first, and was up to his knees in the water before Ernest could reach the place. He threw the oysters to his brother, who put them into his handkerchief: having first secured in his pocket one particularly large shell for his own use.

Fritz not having yet returned, his mother was beginning to be uneasy, when he suddenly appeared holding his hands behind him, with a sort of would-be melancholy air.

'What have you found?' asked his brothers.

'Nothing,' he answered.

But Jack, running behind him, exclaimed:

'A sucking-pig! a sucking-pig!'

Fritz thereupon proudly displayed his prize, which I recognised as an agouti, a little animal rather like a rabbit, and not a sucking-pig, as the boys had supposed. He had shot it in the wood.

Questions were eagerly showered upon him by his brothers, but I spoke seriously to him about the evil habit of lying, even in jest, whereupon he expressed his sorrow.

He then told us that he had passed over to the other side of the river, and had found the shore there quite low, and covered with casks, chests, and planks, and different sorts of things washed up by the sea.

I told him we would go there as soon as possible to secure some of these things, but first we must go back to the ship and try to fetch away the animals.

'If we had the cow we could soak our biscuit in milk,' observed dainty Ernest.

Fritz told us also that he had not seen the smallest trace of man, dead or alive, on land or water.

Our soup was now ready; the boys thereupon tried to open the oysters with their knives, but only succeeded in cutting their own fingers. I showed them how to place the shells near the fire, whereupon they opened of themselves. Then I explained that the oysters were esteemed a great delicacy, and were swallowed raw. They followed my example in holding up the shells and letting the oyster inside slip down their throats; but they made wry faces, and did not seem to appreciate the delicious morsel, for, as they had lived very simply at home, such things were new to them.

Having thus secured a ladle, we all dipped in the pot, but as the shells had no handles, we only succeeded in scalding our fingers, and a chorus of groans followed. Ernest was the only one who had been too cautious to burn himself; he quietly took the shell he had kept for himself, which was as large and deep as a small saucer, from his pocket, and, carefully dipping it into the pot, drew it out filled with as much soup as was his fair share, and set it down till it should cool.

'You have taken good care of yourself,' said I. 'Didn't it occur to you that you might have saved this prize for your mother instead of yourself? As a punishment, I bid you give your dish of soup to the dogs, and yourself share with the rest of us.'

He was instantly ashamed of himself, and placed the shell, filled with soup, upon the ground; in a moment the dogs had licked up every drop. A few minutes elapsed, and while we were eagerly watching the pot we heard a snarl, and, looking round, saw Turk and Flora tearing the agouti to pieces in order to eat him. The boys all screamed together. Fritz seized his gun and struck the dogs with it so hard that he bent it, and his voice was raised so high in his fury that it re-echoed from the rocks.

The dogs ran away terrified, and when Fritz had calmed down a little I pointed out to him the folly and unmanliness of this want of self-control. By this time the soup was cool, and we at last made our meal.

The sun began to sink into the west. The fowls gathered round, pecking here and there at the morsels of biscuit which had fallen on the ground. Then my wife produced the bag she had so mysteriously huddled into the tub, and drawing from it handfuls of grain, scattered them upon the ground for the ducks and hens. Seeing this, I suggested that we should not use anything so valuable so lavishly, but keep it as seed for a future harvest, in which she agreed. Then the pigeons sought a roosting-place among the rocks; the hens ranged themselves in a line along the ridge of the tent; and the geese and ducks betook themselves in a body, cackling and quacking as they proceeded, to a marshy bit of ground near the sea, where some thick bushes afforded them shelter.

A little later we began to follow their example by preparing for bed. First, we loaded our guns and pistols, and laid them carefully in the tent; next, we held evening prayer, and with the last ray of the sun we entered our tent, and, after drawing the sail-cloth over the hooks, to close the entrance, we laid ourselves down on the grass and moss we had previously collected.

The boys noticed with surprise that darkness came down all at once without any twilight. This fact made me suspect we were not far from the equator, where day and night succeed each other very suddenly. Though the day had been hot, the night was quite cold; but we were all so tired that in spite of this we soon fell asleep, and found our first night in the desert island very tolerably comfortable.

CHAPTER III

A VOYAGE OF DISCOVERY

WE were awakened in the morning by the crowing of the cocks, and my wife and I, on talking matters over, agreed that it would be best for me to take Fritz and go in search of any traces of our late shipmates along the shore, while the three younger boys stayed with her for the day. She then laid and lit the fire, and put some water on to boil, while I awoke the rest of the party. When I asked Jack for his lobster, he ran and fetched it from a cleft in the rock, where he had hidden it in case the dogs ate it as they had done Fritz's agouti.

I praised his prudence, and asked if he would give Fritz the great claw to carry with him for his lunch on our journey.

'What journey?' asked all the boys at once. 'We will go too. A journey! a journey!' and they clapped their hands and jumped round me like little kids.

'It is impossible for all of you to go,' I said. 'You three must stay at home to-day and take care of your mother; you shall keep Flora to guard you, while we will take Turk with us. Make haste, Fritz, and see that the guns are ready.'

Jack, who was of a generous spirit, cried out that we should take the whole lobster with us, at which Ernest protested.

'I cannot think why you should give it all to them,' he said. 'You need not be uneasy about their journey. Like Robinson Crusoe, they will be sure to find some coconuts, which they will like much better than your miserable lobster; only think, a fine round nut, Jack, as big as my head, and with at least a teacupful of milk in it!'

'Bring me one, father, will you?' cried little Francis.

We now prepared to set out. We took each a bag for game, and a hatchet. I put a pair of pistols in the leather band round Fritz's waist and took two myself, and we did not forget some biscuit and a flask of fresh river water. At breakfast, when we all attacked the lobster we found it so tough that we were allowed to pack what was left for our journey without further regret from anyone.

Fritz urged me to set out before it grew too hot, in which he was quite right; so, having seen that the guns we left behind were loaded in case of need, we said good-bye and started.

We found we had to go a good way up the river before we could cross, as the banks were high and steep. But at last we passed over on some large rocks that formed stepping-stones, and then forced our way through tall grass which was twined with other plants, and, being half dried by the sun, made the task very difficult.

When we had walked about a hundred paces, we heard a loud noise behind us, and a rustling in the grass, which was almost as tall as ourselves. I thought it might be a serpent, a tiger, or some other ferocious animal. But I was well satisfied with Fritz, who, instead of being frightened and running away, stood still and firm to face the danger. Our alarm was, however, short; for out rushed, not an enemy, but our faithful Turk, whom we had forgotten, but who had quickly followed us.

This incident over, we resumed our walk. On our left was the sea and we kept on along the shore, after having got clear of the tall grass; but though we looked in all directions, we could see no trace of any of the shipwrecked sailors.

Fritz suggested firing his gun from time to time, that, should they be near us, they might know we were there.

But this I objected to, reminding him that the sound might also bring down savages upon us, if there were any in the island, and that it would be as well not to fire unless it was necessary.

When we had gone about four miles, we turned inland and threw ourselves on the ground, by the side of a clear, running stream, and, taking out our food, refreshed ourselves. Presently our attention was attracted by strange noises made by birds in the trees, and when we caught a glimpse of the birds, we saw that their plumage was of brilliant colours.

Fritz also said that he had seen some animals like apes among the bushes, and just then Turk began to bark so loud that the wood resounded with the noise. Fritz, bewildered by so many excitements,

10

sprang up, and as he did so stumbled on a small round body which lay on the ground; he handed it to me, observing that it must be the nest of some bird.

'What makes you think that?' I asked. 'It seems to me much more like a coconut.'

And when he persisted in his opinion, I told him to split it open, in order that we might prove what it was.

This he did, and found I was right; but the nut, alas! from lying on the ground, had rotted, and could not be eaten, and appeared merely like a bit of dried skin.

Fritz was much amused at this.

'How I wish Ernest could have been here!' he cried. 'He envied me the fine large coconuts I was to find, and the whole teacupful of milk which was to spring out from the inside!'

'Never mind,' I said, 'we will find a good one before we go home, and take one to Ernest, too.'

After looking for some time we did really discover another, and on opening it, were delighted to find it tolerably good. It was a little oily and rancid, it is true, yet we enjoyed it, and then went on with our exploration. We pushed our way across the wood, being often obliged to cut a path through the bushes, overrun by creeping plants, with our hatchet. At last we reached a plain, which we crossed before plunging again into a wood on the right.

Here we soon noticed that some of the trees were very curious. Fritz, whose sharp eyes were always on the alert, examined them closely, and was the first to find words to express their oddness.

'What odd trees!' he cried, 'with wens growing all about their trunks!'

I told him that they were of the gourd-tree kind, the trunks of which bear fruit.

Fritz had never heard of such a tree, but he broke off one of the excrescences, and told me it was exactly like a gourd, only the rind was thicker and harder.

'This is a most useful discovery,' I said, 'for now we can make dishes, basins, flasks.'

'Hurrah!' cried the boy gleefully; 'we need not scald our fingers any more by using those wretched oyster-shells.'

'Negro savages set as much value on the rind of this fruit as on gold,' I told him. 'These rinds serve them as vessels for their food and drink, and sometimes they are even used for cooking.'

11

'Oh, father! that must be impossible,' he argued, 'for the heat of fire would soon burn them up.'

'I did not say the rind was put upon the fire.'

'I don't see how they could do it any other way.'

'Well, I believe the method is as follows: Some water is put into half of one of these rinds, and into the water some fish, or a crab, or anything else there is to be cooked. Then some red hot stones are thrown in one by one, so that the water gets hot and boils the food.'

Fritz was much interested, and very anxious to try; and, though it was hardly the time for this, I told him that at any rate he should see me make some plates and dishes. I tied a bit of string round the middle of the gourd as tight as possible, striking it pretty hard with the handle of my knife, and I drew it tighter and tighter till the gourd fell apart, forming two regular-shaped bowls or vessels.

Fritz was astonished and delighted.

'These are capital dishes,' he cried. 'But I cannot imagine, father, how you can make a flask from a gourd.'

'That is more difficult,' I said, 'and needs preparation a long time beforehand. The negroes bind a piece of string, linen, bark of a tree, or anything they can get, round the part of a gourd nearest the stalk while it is still very young and growing, so that as the plant increases in size the bandaged part remains small, and in this way flasks or bottles of a very good shape are made.'

While we were talking, we had both been busy splitting more gourds. These I filled with sand, to prevent their shrinking, and left them for the sun to dry thoroughly. We intended to pick them up on our way back.

After this we walked on for a long time until we arrived at a spot where a strip of land stretched far out into the sea, and on it was some high ground or a hill. We made directly for this, and on reaching the top we saw a scene of wild and solitary beauty, stretching out in all directions; but in vain we used our telescopes: we could see no trace of man. By this time the heat of the sun was very great, and we felt we must again seek the shelter of trees, or we could not endure it.

So when we descended the hill we made our way to a wood of palms, and were glad to get into the shade again. Our path was clothed with reeds and entwined with other plants, which made progress difficult, so we advanced slowly and cautiously, fearing that snakes might be concealed, and we made Turk go before, to give us notice of anything dangerous. I also cut a reed-stalk for defence, but I had not held

12

it many minutes before I found my hand covered with a sticky juice, which, when I tasted it, proved to be very sweet, so that I realized we were actually walking in a grove of sugar-canes. I did not tell Fritz, for I wanted him to find out for himself; so I simply called out to him to cut a stick for himself as I had done. This he did, and as he swung it in all directions, soon felt the sticky juice upon his hands. And hardly a second after the truth dawned upon him, and he cried out joyfully:

'Father, father! I have found some sugar! I have a sugar-cane in my hand!'

He kept sucking the juice of the single cane he had cut with great joy, and, when he was satisfied, expressed his intention of cutting a great bundle of canes to carry home to the others.

'I have no objection,' I said; 'but do not take too heavy a load.'

Counsel was given in vain. He persisted in cutting at least a dozen of the largest canes, tore off their leaves, tied them together, and, putting them under his arm, dragged them, as well as he was able, to the end of the plantation. After this we returned by a circuit to the first wood, where we had found the coconuts, and here we settled down to rest a little while. We had scarcely seated, however, when a number of large monkeys, terrified by the sight of us and the barking of Turk, stole nimbly up the palm-trees, and, fixing their eyes upon us, ground their teeth and made horrible grimaces, screaming at us all the time. Fritz prepared to shoot at them instantly. He threw his burdens on the ground, and it was with difficulty I could prevent him from firing.

'Ah, father, why did not you let me fire? Monkeys are such malicious, mischievous animals! Look how they are grinning at us!'

I laughed at this and told him to stand aside, for an idea had come into my head, and I meant to put it to the test.

Accordingly I began to throw some stones at the monkeys, and though I could not throw them half high enough, they answered the purpose, for, with their usual mimicry, the monkeys furiously tore off all the coconuts within their reach and hurled them down upon us, so that it was with difficulty we avoided being hit by them. In a short time all the ground around us was covered with coconuts.

Fritz laughed heartily at the success of the stratagem, and as the shower of coconuts began to subside, we gathered them up, and having first enjoyed the milk through the three small holes, where we found it easy to insert the point of a knife, we opened the shells with a hatchet. The milk of the coconut has not a pleasant flavour, but it is excellent for quenching thirst. What we liked best was a kind of solid

13

cream which adheres to the shell, and which we scraped off. We mixed with it a little of the sap of our sugar-canes, and found this delicious.

These coconuts were certainly very superior to the one that we had at first picked up, being fresh and in fine condition. After this we gave poor Turk the rest of the lobster and what biscuit we had over, feeling we did not want it. He ate up every scrap and intimated he would have liked more, but we had nothing else to give him.

As we prepared to start once more, I tied all the coconuts, which had stalks, together, and threw them across my shoulder. Fritz resumed his bundle of sugar-canes. We divided the rest of the things between us, and continued our way towards home.

CHAPTER IV

A NIGHT ALARM

FRITZ now began to show signs of weariness; the sugar-canes galled his shoulders, and he was obliged to shift them often. At last he stopped to take breath.

'I never could have thought,' he said, 'that a few sugar-canes could be so heavy. I pity the poor negroes who carry heavy loads of them! Yet I must go on, for I long to see mother and Ernest eating them.'

After a while, noticing that I sucked the cane I was carrying, he tried to do the same in order to refresh himself. It was in vain, however; scarcely a drop of the sap reached his eager lips.

'Why,' said he, 'though the cane is full of juice, I cannot get any.'

'Try to think for yourself,' I replied.

This he did, and presently announced that by making a little hole in the cane above the knot he could get at the juice by sucking the end.

I asked him to explain to me why this happened, and after further thought, he answered correctly that in sucking the juice the air in the mouth was exhausted; the external air, pressing at the same time through the hole, filled this void; the juice of the cane formed an obstacle to this effort, and was accordingly driven into the mouth.

I was pleased to find he could reason the thing out for himself, and warned him not to carry out the plan too effectually, or he might only have a bundle of empty canes to present to those at home; however, as the juice of the sugar-cane is apt to turn sour soon after cutting, especially in such heat, this mattered the less.

'At least,' said Fritz, 'I will take the others some of the coconut milk with which I filled my flask.'

'In this, too, I think you will be disappointed. You talk of milk, but the milk of the coconut, when exposed to the air and heat, turns soon to vinegar.'

'Oh, heavens, how provoking! I must taste it this very minute,' he cried anxiously.

The flask was lowered from his shoulder and the stopper unscrewed; then the contents of the bottle burst upwards, hissing and frothing like champagne.

'Bravo, Mr. Fritz!' I cried. 'Your milk has turned to wine; don't let it make you tipsy.'

'Oh, taste it, father, taste it! it is quite nice; not the least like vinegar; it is rather like wine: its taste is sweet, and it is so sparkling! Don't you think it is good? If all the milk turns like this, it will be even better than I thought.'

Soon after this we reached the place where we had left our gourd dishes upon the sand; we found them perfectly dry and as hard as bone, so we added them to our loads and trudged on.

Scarcely had we passed through the little wood in which we had lunched when Turk dashed into the middle of a troop of monkeys, and seized one of them who held a young one in her arms. Before we could stop him he had killed her.

Fritz flew to prevent the deed. He lost his hat, and threw down all he was carrying, but he was too late to save the monkey.

However, the young one, who was quite unhurt, sprang nimbly on his shoulders, and fastened its feet in his curly hair; nor could the squalls of Fritz nor all the shaking he gave it make it let go its hold.

I laughed heartily at the boy's face of dismay under the sudden onslaught.

'Perhaps,' I said, 'it adopts you for a father, having lost its mother.'

By this time Fritz had recovered from his fright, and disengaged the little animal gently. It was not larger than a kitten, and quite unable to help itself.

'Father,' cried Fritz, 'do let me have it for my own. I will take the greatest care of it; I will give it all my share of the milk of the coconuts till we get our cows and goats.'

I agreed readily to this, for I was pleased with his behaviour.

So we started once more, and I carried the bundle of sugar-canes, while the little monkey sat on Fritz's shoulder. Whenever Turk came near, however, it trembled and shrunk closer up to its new master.

Fritz was angry with the dog for having killed the mother monkey, and finally decided that it was only fair that he should carry the child; so he produced some string, and, making the monkey sit on the dog's back, tied it there with some string. At first the monkey seemed frightened, but after being petted and caressed it sat quite quietly, and seemed perfectly comfortable. Turk also made some objections, but, partly by scolding and partly by caresses, we succeeded in quieting him, and he consented to carry the little burden. Fritz put another piece of string round Turk's neck, by which he might lead him. All this caused delay, for I must confess we had not hurried much, and I knew that they would be eagerly expecting our return at home. I smiled at the idea that we should look like a couple of travelling showmen, a notion that amused Fritz when I told it to him.

'Jack is fond of making faces,' said he; 'he can learn a few more from my wee monkey.'

We had not time for much more anticipation before we found ourselves on the bank of the river not far from home. Flora from the other side announced our approach by a violent barking, and Turk replied so heartily that the little monkey in its fright jumped the length of its string on to Fritz's shoulder. Turk, being released, ran off to greet his companion, and shortly after all the family appeared in sight, showing their joy at our safe return. They made their way along the river on one side and we on the other, till we had reached the place we crossed in the morning.

Then we re-crossed, and heard their happy exclamations.

'A monkey! a live monkey! Oh, what fun! How did you catch him? What a droll face he has!'

'He is very ugly,' said little Francis, half afraid to touch him.

'He is much prettier than you,' retorted Jack, 'only see, he is laughing! I wish I could see him eat.'

'Ah, if we had but some coconuts!' cried Ernest. 'Could you not find any?'

'Have you brought me any coconut milk ?' asked Francis.

Then, noticing the sugar-canes, coconuts, and gourds, they broke forth again in a chorus, though they had not the least idea what these things were.

Questions and exclamations succeeded each other with such rapidity as to leave no time to answer them.

At length, when all became a little quieter, I answered that we had had a fortunate day and made many wonderful discoveries, but had seen no trace of our shipmates whom we had gone out to seek.

Then the boys all hastened to relieve us of the loads we carried. Jack took my gun, Ernest the coconuts, Francis the gourd-rinds, and my wife my game-bag. Fritz distributed the sugar-canes and put his monkey on the back of Turk, to the great amusement of the children, at the same time begging Ernest to carry his gun. But Ernest, who was always lazy, assured him that the large, heavy bowls with which he was loaded were as much as he had strength to carry. His mother, a little too indulgent, at once took them herself, and thus we walked to our tent.

Fritz whispered to me that if Ernest had known what the large, heavy bowls were, he would not so readily have parted with them. Then, turning to his brother, he cried:

'Why, Ernest, do you know that these bowls are coconuts — your dear coconuts — and full of the milk you talked so much about?'

'What?' cried Ernest in astonishment. 'Oh, give them to me, mother — I will carry them; and I can carry the gun too.'

'No, no, Ernest,' answered his mother, 'you shall not tease us with any more of your longdrawn sighs about fatigue; after a hundred yards you would begin again.'

Ernest would willingly have asked her to give him the coconuts in exchange for the gun, but this he was ashamed to do; so, as he happened to be carrying the sugar-canes too, an idea occurred to him.

'I have only,' he said, 'to get rid of these sticks, then I can carry the gun in my hand.'

'I would advise you not to find the sticks heavy, either,' said Fritz dryly; 'you will be sorry if you do, for, as it happens, they are sugar-canes!'

'Sugar-canes! sugar-canes!' exclaimed all the boys at once, and, surrounding Fritz, made him tell them exactly how to suck the juice out.

My wife also was quite astonished and much interested, so I told her about all our treasures. She was by far the most delighted with the plates and dishes, because they were indispensably necessary.

By this time we had reached our camp, and saw with pleasure the preparations for a good supper. On one side of the fire was a turnspit, which my wife had made by driving two forked pieces of wood into the ground and placing a long stick, sharpened at one end, across

17

them. By this invention she could roast fish or other food with the help of little Francis, who was entrusted with the care of turning it round from time to time. She had prepared a bird that looked like a goose, the fat of which ran down into some oyster-shells placed there to serve as a dripping-pan. There was, besides, a dish of fish, which the boys had caught; and the iron pot was upon the fire filled with soup, which smelt excellent. Near at hand stood one of the casks which we had recovered from the sea; this had been opened, and was full of Dutch cheeses. All this was hardly what one would expect to see on a desert island, and was very acceptable to two tired explorers.

The bird I discovered was not a goose, but, as Ernest assured me, a sort of penguin, which he had knocked down with a stick.

'It is a very stupid bird,' he added, 'and so slow; it never tried to run away, and sits in one position for hours together, as if it were thinking deeply, and looks like a sack on end. I think it must be the kind called the Stupid Penguin.'

I began asking further questions, in order to draw out the boy's powers of observation, but my wife interrupted me, asking that this discussion might be postponed, in order that, instead of talking about the bird, we could begin to eat him.

At this moment Jack broke in upon us, crying out that he had tried to make the little monkey eat, offering it everything he could think of, but that it would not touch anything. I suggested that they should try it with some of the milk from the coconuts. This they did, and each boy in turn amused himself with making it suck the corner of his pocket handkerchief dipped in the milk of the coconut. The monkey seemed pleased with this food, and I began to hope we might rear it. We decided to call it Nip.

The boys were beginning to break some more of the nuts with the hatchet, after having drawn out the milk through the three little holes, when I told them to stop and to bring me a saw. The thought had struck me that, by dividing the nuts carefully, the two halves, when scooped out, would make teacups or basins, which would be very useful in addition to our gourd-bowls. Jack, who was always the quickest, brought me the saw. With this I divided the nuts, and soon we each had a new cup; and I firmly believe that never did the most magnificent service of china give half the pleasure to its possessor that these rough cups and bowls, which we had made ourselves from gourds and coconuts, gave to us. Fritz suddenly remembered the wine in his flask, but when he tasted it, he made a wry face and said it was like vinegar.

'What! vinegar?' exclaimed my wife. 'How lucky! it will make sauce for our bird, mixed with the fat which has fallen from it in roasting.'

No sooner said than done. This vinegar certainly improved the rather fishy flavour of the penguin, and our fish also. It amused me, meanwhile, to hear the talk among the boys, for each one boasted of what he had himself contributed to our meal. It was Jack and Francis who had caught the fish in one of the shallows, while Ernest, with very little trouble to himself, secured his penguin. As a matter of fact, my wife had done the hardest work of all in rolling the cask of Dutch cheeses from the shore and then breaking it open.

By the time we had finished the sun was nearly setting, and, remembering how quickly the darkness would fall, we hastened to get ready for bed. My wife had collected a quantity of dry grass, which she had spread in the tent, so that we had a prospect of being much more comfortable than the night before. The fowls went to roost as they had done the preceding evening. We said our prayers, and went into the tent, taking with us the young monkey, who was a favourite with all. Fritz and Jack, indeed, quarrelled as to which of them should enjoy the honour of his company for the night, and it was at last decided that he should lie between them. I fastened the sail-cloth in front of the tent, and then, quite tired out by all I had done, I lay down on the soft grass with the others, and was soon sound asleep.

However, it was not long before I woke with a violent start, hearing the fowls fluttering about on the roof of the tent and the two dogs barking loudly. I sprang to my feet, and, seizing a gun, went to look out, followed by my wife and Fritz.

The dogs continued barking with the same violence, and at intervals even howled. We had hardly stepped out of the tent when, to our surprise, we saw by the light of the moon a terrible scene: at least a dozen jackals had set upon our brave dogs, who defended themselves desperately. Already the dogs had disabled one or two, and those that remained were snarling and whining.

I was relieved to see it was nothing worse.

'We shall soon set these fellows at rest,' I said. 'Let us fire both together, my boy; but take care how you aim, for fear of killing the dogs.'

We fired, and one of the jackals instantly fell dead upon the sand. The others, terrified by the unexpected noise, scampered away. Turk and Flora raced after them, and so the matter ended. Fritz asked me to let him drag the dead jackal towards the tent, that he might exhibit it the next morning to his brothers. I thought, however, that Turk and

Flora might want to eat it, and advised him to leave it. However, he was anxious to try to keep it, and pulled it up near a rock by the entrance to the tent.

Oddly enough, the younger boys slept so soundly that they had not even been awakened by the firing of the guns. So we lay down by their side till day began to break.

CHAPTER V

FRITZ AND I VISIT THE WRECK

As soon as I woke in the morning, seeing that my wife was already awake, I began to discuss with her our plans for the day. Two things were absolutely necessary, the first to fetch the live-stock from the ship, which might at any moment break up, and the second to build ourselves a better sort of house.

Having agreed that the voyage to the ship was the more important, I resolved to take Fritz with me, as on the day before, leaving the other three boys with their mother. When we had decided this, springing to my feet, I cried out loudly:

'Get up, boys — get up! we have important work to do to-day.'

At these words Fritz jumped up, and, running out of the tent, found the dead jackal still untouched, but quite stiff. So, in the spirit of mischief, he fixed him in the sand, right opposite the tent door, as if he were taking a walk.

Jack was the first of the others to appear, with the young monkey on his shoulder; but when the little creature saw the jackal, he sprang away in terror, and hid himself in the corner of the tent, pulling the dry grass over him, so as to hide himself completely.

The younger boys gave vent to a chorus of exclamations at the sight.

'It is a wolf!' cried Francis, rather frightened.

'No, no,' said Jack, going near the jackal, and taking one of his paws; 'it is a yellow dog, and he is dead.'

'It is neither a dog nor a wolf,' interrupted Ernest in a conceited tone. 'Do you not see that it is the golden fox ?'

Fritz burst out laughing.

'With all your reading, Mr. Professor,' he said, 'you can't tell a jackal when you see one.'

20

'No one is wrong,' I interposed, to prevent a quarrel, 'for a jackal is really very nearly akin to a dog and a wolf as well as a fox.'

This settled the little dispute, and we all turned eagerly to discuss the more important question of breakfast. Alas! there was nothing but dry biscuit. Fritz asked for a piece of cheese to eat with it, and Ernest looked eagerly at the second cask we had pulled out of the sea to discover whether it also contained Dutch cheeses. In a minute he came up to us, joy sparkling in his eyes.

'Father,' said he, 'if we had a little butter spread upon our biscuit, don't you think it would improve it?'

'That indeed it would; but *if* — *if* — ' I asked rather impatiently: 'What do you mean?'

'Well,' he said triumphantly, 'this barrel is full of salt butter. I made a little opening in it with a knife, and see, I got out enough to spread upon a piece of biscuit.'

'Your greediness is of some general use,' I remarked. 'Who will have some butter on his biscuit ?'

The boys surrounded the cask in a moment, while I was in some perplexity as to how to break it open. Fritz was for taking of the topmost hoop, and thus loosening one of the ends. But this I objected to, knowing that the great heat of the sun would melt the butter, which would then run out and be wasted. The idea occurred to me that I might make a hole in the bottom of the cask large enough to allow us to scoop out the butter, and I set about making a little wooden shovel to use for the purpose. All this was very successful. I used my wooden shovel as a scoop, and drew out enough butter to fill half a coconut shell. Then we toasted our biscuit, and while it was hot spread the butter on it, and made a hearty breakfast.

'One of the things we must not forget to look for in the ship,' said Fritz, 'is a spiked collar for our dogs, to protect them if they fight with wild beasts.'

'Oh,' said Jack, 'I can make spiked collars if mother will help me.'

She agreed readily; but Jack would not tell us his plan just then, saying it was a secret.

Then I told Fritz that he was to come with me to the ship, and he ran down to get the boat ready. While he was doing so I looked about for a pole, and tied a piece of white linen to the end of it; then I drove it into the ground, in a place where we could see it from the ship, and I told my wife that, in case of any accident, she must take down the pole and fire a gun three times as a signal of distress. But I told her at the

21

same time it was very likely we should stay away all night if we were not summoned back, for we should have a great deal to do.

We took nothing with us but our guns and some powder and shot, knowing we should find provisions on board; yet I agreed to carry with us the young monkey, so that we could give it some milk from the cow or from a goat.

We set off in silence, watching the figures on shore growing smaller and smaller. Fritz rowed steadily, and I did my best to help him by rowing from time to time with the oar which served me for a rudder.

We had to rest at intervals, but at last we ran into a current, made by the flow of the river into the sea, and this carried us easily out. So eventually we found ourselves safely at the side of the ship, and could fasten our boat securely to one of its timbers.

Fritz went at once, with his young monkey on his arm, to the main deck, where he found all the animals we had left on board assembled. They all showed pleasure at our arrival, though they were not hungry, having still some of the food and water we had left them remaining. The first thing we did was to put the young monkey to one of the goats, that he might suck for himself; and this he did with such evident pleasure and such odd grimaces that he afforded us much amusement.

Fritz and I then consulted what should be our first occupation. To my surprise, he suggested that we should put up a sail in our boat.

'What makes you think of such a thing just now,' I asked, 'when we have so many things of greater importance to arrange?'

'True, father,' said Fritz; 'but I found it very difficult to row for so long. I noticed, too, that, though the wind blew strongly in my face, the current still carried us on. Now, as the current will be of no use on our way back, I was thinking that we might make the wind do the work. Our boat will be very heavy when we have loaded it with all the things we mean to take away, and I am afraid I shall not be strong enough to row to land; so do you not think that a sail would be a good thing?'

I thought there was reason in this, and agreed to try to make a sail.

We found a pole strong enough for a mast, and another, not so thick, for a cross-piece. I then went to the sail-room, and cut a large sail down to a triangular shape; I made holes along the edges and passed cords through them. We then got a pulley, and with this and some rope we fastened the sail to the mast, which we rigged up by nailing a board with a hole in it across one of the tubs of our boat and so fixing it.

Fritz, after taking observations through a telescope of what was

22

passing on land, told me all seemed well — he could even see his mother walking about.

But our work with the sail had taken us a long time, and, with all we had yet to do, I saw we should certainly have to pass the night on board, as I had expected, and not join the others on shore that day.

We employed the rest of the day in emptying the tubs of the useless ballast of stones which we had brought in them, and putting in their place nails, pieces of cloth, and different kinds of utensils. We also secured knives and forks and spoons, and in the captain's cabin we found some services of silver and a little chest filled with bottles of wine.

We next descended to the kitchen, which we stripped of gridirons, kettles, and pots of all kinds, including a small roasting jack. Our last prize was a chest of choice eatables, containing hams, sausages, and other savoury food. I took good care not to forget some little sacks of maize, of wheat, and other grain, and some potatoes. We next added such implements for gardening as we could find — shovels, hoes, spades, and rakes. Fritz reminded me that we had found sleeping on the ground both cold and hard, so we took as well some hammocks and blankets. He also brought a few books from the captain's library, including some volumes on Natural History and a Bible. The last articles were a barrel of sulphur, a quantity of ropes, some small string, and a large roll of sail-cloth. The vessel appeared to us to be in so wretched a condition that the least wind must send her to pieces, so we felt that we must make the most of our time.

Our cargo was so large that the tubs were filled to the very brim, except the first and last, which we kept for ourselves.

Night surprised us with its suddenness, and we saw almost at once a large blazing fire on the shore, which was the signal we had agreed upon if all was well. We tied four lanterns to our mast-head in answer, and then, after saying our prayers, settled down to rest.

23

CHAPTER VI

THE ANIMALS SWIM ASHORE

ALMOST as soon as it was light I was looking eagerly through the captain's telescope at the shore, and had the satisfaction of seeing my wife come out of the tent and walk down to the beach. Then, waking Fritz, we soon settled down to a breakfast of biscuit and ham.

'Now,' I said, when we had finished, 'we shall have to think how we can get these animals ashore.'

'Would it be possible to make a raft?' asked Fritz.

'But how could we induce a cow, a donkey, and a sow to get upon a raft, or to remain quiet on it?'

'The sow is so fat, she would float,' he said; 'and I believe the others would swim with very little trouble if we could give them swimming-belts.'

I laughed at the idea, but fixed a belt on one of the lambs as a trial, and found that after the first plunge into the water it floated very well.

I had taken the precaution of tying a string to the lamb, with which I now drew it back to the ship.

We next got two small empty tubs, and nailed a large piece of sail-cloth across from one to the other, and added some leather straps. Then I fixed this contrivance on the donkey, so that a tub was on each side, the sail-cloth beneath him, and the straps passed over him to hold it in place. This seemed likely to do so well that I made the same kind of harness for the cow.

It was now the turn of the smaller animals: of these, the sow gave us the most trouble; we were first obliged to put a muzzle on her to prevent her biting, and then we tied a large piece of cork under her body. The sheep and goats were quieter, but we had much hard work before we had fitted them all with something which should support them in the water. When every one was equipped, we tied a cord to either the horns or the neck of each animal, and to the other end of the cord a piece of wood, so that we could take hold of the ropes and draw the animals to us if it should be necessary. We began our experiments with the donkey, by taking him to the edge of the ship and then suddenly shoving him off. He fell into the water, and for a moment disappeared; but we soon saw him rise and begin to strike out.

Next came the cow's turn, and as she was infinitely more valuable than the donkey, I was more afraid of losing her. We pushed her overboard, however, and she reached the water safely; when there, she did not sink so low, and she made her way toward the land with gravity, and, if I may so express it, a sort of dignified composure. So one by one we threw all the animals into the water, where by-and-by they appeared floating at their ease, and seemingly quite happy. The sow was the only exception. She became furious, set up a loud squalling, and struggled with much violence in the water. We had now not a moment to lose. We sprang into our boat, and were soon in the midst of our farmyard. We carefully gathered all the floating bits of wood at the end of the strings, so soon as we could reach them, and fastened them to the stern of the boat. When everything was fixed, we hoisted our sail, which luckily acted well enough, and the wind, being in the right direction, blew us along merrily.

We now saw how impossible it would have been for us to row to such a distance without the aid of a sail; especially as the weight of so many animals sank the boat very low in the water. We laughed heartily, however, at the queer spectacle we must present dragging after us such an odd team; and in high spirits we made an excellent dinner. Afterwards Fritz amused himself with the monkey, while I was occupied in thinking of those I had left on land, whom I now tried to see through my telescope. While I was thus engaged a sudden exclamation from Fritz filled me with alarm.

'Oh, heavens!' he cried, 'we are lost! a huge fish is coming up to the boat. It must be a shark!'

'And why lost ?' said I, half angry. 'Be ready with your gun, and the moment he is close upon us we will fire.'

He had nearly reached the boat, and with the rapidity of lightning had seized the foremost sheep.

At this instant we both fired, so that the shots hit the head of the monster simultaneously. The shark half turned round in the water, and hurried off to sea, leaving the water red, which convinced us he had been severely wounded.

As soon as this adventure was over, I resumed the rudder, and as the wind drove us straight towards the bay, I took down the sail, and continued rowing till we reached a convenient spot for our cattle to land, which they did without difficulty.

I had already been surprised and uneasy at finding none of the family looking out for us on the shore; but now my wife and the boys were soon with us, eager to greet us. When the first burst of happiness at meeting had subsided, we all sat down on the grass, and I gave them an account of what we had done. My wife could find no words to express her surprise and joy at seeing so many useful animals round us, and this increased our satisfaction.

I gave Fritz full credit for his help and suggestions, and saw him flush with pleasure to be so much praised.

Ernest and Jack now ran to the boat and shouted their admiration of the mast and the sail. Then we began to unpack our cargo, while Jack stole aside and amused himself with the animals, taking off the jackets from the sheep and goats, bursting from time to time into shouts of laughter at the ridiculous figure of the donkey, who stood before them adorned with his two casks and his swimming apparatus, and braying loud enough to make us deaf.

By-and-by I noticed with surprise that Jack had round his waist a belt of yellow skin, in which were fixed two pistols. I asked him where he got it from.

'I made it myself,' he replied. 'Look at the dogs, too, and see what I made for them.'

I did so, and saw that each of them had on a collar similar to the belt round Jack's waist, with, however, the exception that the collars were armed with nails, the points of which were outwards and looked very alarming. 'And is it you, Jack,' cried I, 'who have invented and made these collars and your belt?'

'Yes, father, but mother helped me a little with the sewing,' he answered.

'Where did you get the leather and the thread and the needle?'

'Fritz's jackal furnished the first,' answered my wife; 'and as to the last, have I not an enchanted bag from which I can draw out such articles as I want ? So if you have a particular fancy for any thing, you have only to tell me.'

Fritz, meantime, was looking sulky at the fact that Jack had cut the jackal's skin into strips, for he considered it his own prize. He, however, concealed his ill-humour as well as he could; but presently he called out suddenly, holding his nose as he spoke, 'What a filthy smell!'

'Yes,' said Jack quietly, 'it comes from my belt, but it will be all right when it dries,' and he danced about, not minding it in the least himself, until even Fritz had to laugh and forget his ill-humour.

Being now very hungry, I told Fritz to bring us the Westphalia ham.

'A ham!' cried they all. 'Oh, what a treat!'

'You shall have an omelette to eat with it,' my wife remarked, and

26

showed us about a dozen turtle's eggs, and then hurried away to cook them.

'I found them,' said Ernest. 'They are the very same that Robinson Crusoe found in his island! They are like white balls, covered with a skin like wetted parchment, and they were buried in the sand upon the shore.'

It was now time to make a movement, so with the help of the boys I unharnessed the remainder of the animals and returned to the tent.

In the meanwhile my wife had prepared the omelette, and spread a table-cloth on the end of the cask of butter, upon which she had placed some of the plates and silver spoons we had brought from the ship. The ham was in the middle, and the omelette and the cheese opposite to each other; altogether a royal supper for a desert island. By-and-by the two dogs, the fowls, the pigeons, the sheep, and the goats had all assembled round us. It did not please the geese and ducks to come too, for they had found a marshy swamp where there were little crabs in abundance; these they ate eagerly.

When we had finished our supper I told Fritz to open a bottle of Canary wine, which we had brought from the Captain's cabin, for dessert. The boys now dispersed to attend to and pet the animals, while my wife told us what had happened on the island while we were away. She made us laugh by her account of Jack's earnestness in the dirty task of stripping the skin from the dead jackal, and of Ernest's fastidiousness. She explained that Jack had originated the idea of putting the large flat-headed nails through the skin with the points out-wards to form defensive collars for the dogs; and that at his request she had sewed a piece of sail-cloth on the inner side of the collars as lining, both to keep the nails in place and to prevent their heads from chafing the dogs' necks.

This was the first day. On the second day the heat of the sun had been very trying, and she had felt so great a longing to get out of its glare she had decided to make a little expedition into the woods across the river to see whether she could not find some place more suitable for a camp than the bare, rocky seashore. The boys were of course delighted to go with her; and the whole party sallied out, Jack and Ernest carrying guns.

'I thought,' she said, 'how merciful it was that you had taught the boys to use firearms from their earliest years, for many boys of their age would hardly know one end of a gun from the other, yet now I must depend upon my two young sons of thirteen and fourteen for protection in many dangers. The river was difficult to cross, Ernest

27

hopped over on large stones, I carried little Francis on my back and followed him, while Jack plunged boldly in, seeming rather to enjoy the cold water than not. The long grass on the other side was very difficult to get through — in places it was over the dogs' heads. I kept my eye upon them, however, and noticed that Jack was loitering a little behind, and I turned to see what he was doing. I saw him tearing up handfuls of grass, and wiping his clothes with them, and then shaking his pocket-handkerchief and laying it on his shoulders to dry.

"'Oh, mother," said he, when he saw me looking, "I believe all the water of the river has got into my pockets; only see, everything I had in them is wet — pistols, everything."

"'Good gracious!" I interrupted, in great alarm, "had you put your pistols in your pocket? They were not loaded, I hope?"

"'I do not know, mother; I only put them there while my belt was drying, that I might always have them about me."

"'They might have gone off and killed you!" I cried, thinking how a short time ago it was since I had been congratulating myself on his being accustomed to firearms.

"'There is nothing to fear this time," he said, holding the pistols so as to let the water run out of them; and I saw, indeed, there was little danger of their going off, for they had been most thoroughly wet.

'While we were talking we were interrupted by a sudden noise, and saw a large bird flying up from the thickest part of the grass. Both boys prepared to fire, but before they were ready the bird was out of reach. Ernest was bitterly disappointed, crying:

"'What a pity! If the bird had not flown so fast I should have killed him."

"The mischief was, no doubt, that you did not let him know beforehand that you wanted him to wait till you were ready," I observed, laughing.

"'But, mother, how could I possibly suppose that the bird could fly away in less than the twinkling of an eye? Ah, if one would but come at this very moment!'"

"'A good sportsman, Ernest, always holds himself in readiness, for birds do not send messages to give notice of their coming."

"'I wish I knew," said Jack, "what bird it was; I never saw any like it."

"'I am sure it was an eagle," said little Francis, 'for I have read in my book of fables, that an eagle can carry off a sheep, and this bird was terribly large."

"'Oh, yes!" said Ernest scoffingly, "as if all large birds must be

28

eagles! Why, there are some birds much larger even than eagles! The ostrich, for instance. But I must say I should like to have examined this bird closely."

"'If you had had time to examine him, you would have had time to kill him," said I; " but the opportunity is gone."

'As I spoke, a second bird, exactly like the first, except that he was a little larger, rushed out with a great noise and mounted high above their heads.

"'The boys stared with round eyes and open mouths, while I burst out laughing.

"'Oh! what fine sportsmen!" cried I; "they will never let us be in want of game. 'Ah! if one would but come at this very moment!"'

'Ernest was so mortified that he began to cry, while Jack took off his hat, made a profound bow, and roared out, as if for the bird to hear:

"'Have the goodness, Mr. Traveller, to indulge me once more with a little visit, only for a single minute; you cannot imagine what good sort of people we are. I entreat that we may have the pleasure of seeing you once again."

'We now minutely examined the place from which the birds had flown, and found a kind of large nest formed of dry plants, of clumsy workmanship. The nest was empty, with the exception of some broken shells of eggs, showing that the young had not been long hatched; indeed, we heard some rustling in the grass which told us they were not far off, but we could not see them.

'We next reached a little wood, and I do not think you can have been there, for the trees were so enormous that you could not have helped noticing and remarking on them. The odd part about them was, what appeared to us at a distance to be a wood was only a group of about fourteen of them, the trunks of which seemed to be supported in their upright position by arches on each side, these arches being formed by the roots of the tree.

'Jack climbed with considerable trouble upon one of these arch-formed roots, and, with a packthread in his hand measured the actual circumference of the tree itself. He found that it was about thirty feet. It seemed to me that, if it could be managed, a tent or camp of some sort in one of these trees would be a safer and more comfortable refuge than our present tent. The twigs of the tree are strong and thick; its leaves moderately large in size, and rather like those of the hazel tree; but I was unable to discover that it bore any fruit. Immediately under its branches grew in great abundance a short thick kind of plant.

It was so shady under this great dome of leaves that I resolved to go no further, but to enjoy its delicious coolness till it should be time to return.

'A stream flowed at our feet. As it seemed just the place for lunch, we opened the bags we had brought, and enjoyed ourselves exceedingly. Our dogs joined us, but to my great surprise they did not ask for anything to eat, but lay down quietly, and were soon asleep at our feet. When we were quite rested we set out on our return, again keeping close to the river, and eventually we came down to the sea-shore.

'Our dogs immediately began to catch crabs, which they drew with their paws to the shore as the waves washed them up, and then ate with every sign of pleasure. I now understood how it was they had not been hungry at lunch-time, and was pleased to think that they could provide for themselves.

'Ernest, who had wandered ahead by himself, now gave a shout, saying he had found some "turtles' eggs."

'They were partly buried in the sand, but Flora had directed his attention to them by scratching at them. Altogether we collected about two dozen of them, which we placed in our provision bags.

'Just then we saw your sail, and hurried on so as to meet you when you landed.'

The thing which had particularly struck me in this interesting account was the discovery of the great trees.

'And you think we could set up a tent in one of those giant trees at a great height from the ground!' I cried. 'And how are we to get up and down?'

'Don't you remember,' my wife asked, 'the large lime-tree in the public walk of our own town; and the pretty little room which had been built among its branches, and the flight of stairs which led to it? Why should we not make something of the same kind?'

I confessed that it might be possible, though the difficulties of the undertaking seemed to me enormous. However, darkness was falling fast, and so, calling the boys, we prepared to spend another night in our tent.

CHAPTER VII

AN ADVENTURE WITH A SHARK

WHEN my wife and I woke next morning we began at once talking about making a change of abode.

Personally, I thought we were better where we were, but she argued that the intense heat of the sands was getting insupportable; that by remaining here we lost all hope of finding fruits of any kind, and must live on oysters, or on such wild birds as came near us.

And when I pointed out we ought to remain where we could most easily reach the ship, from which we might still bring many things, she replied that we might continue to go to and from the ship, if we wished, from another place as easily as here, but for her part she should not be sorry if we never went again, for she was in an agony of anxiety the whole time we were away. I agreed, therefore, to think seriously of the matter; but said we must first contrive a storehouse among the rocks for our provisions and other things, and next we must throw a bridge across the river, if we were to pass it with all our family and baggage.

'A bridge!' exclaimed my wife; 'if we stay while you build a bridge, we may consider ourselves as fixed for life. Why should we not cross the river as we did before? The ass and the cow will carry all we possess upon their backs.'

I insisted, however, that a bridge was necessary if we wished to keep our stores dry.

'Well, then, a bridge let there be,' said my wife, 'and you will leave our stock of gunpowder here, I hope; for I am never happy with it so near us: a thunder-storm, or some thoughtless action of one of the boys, might bring about a serious explosion.'

This I agreed was very sensible; we need only take what we wanted from time to time.

So when we woke the boys our plans were already made. They were delighted to hear that a bridge was to be built, and still more so that we might in time go to live under the giant trees — a place which they at once christened 'The Promised Land.'

We now began to look about for breakfast, Fritz taking care not to neglect his monkey, who sucked one of the goats as contentedly as if she had been its mother. My wife undertook to milk another, and then the cow, and afterwards she gave some of the milk to each of the chil-

31

dren. The rest she put into one of the flasks, so that we could take it with us.

While this was going on I was getting the boat ready for another journey to the ship, to bring away planks and timbers for the bridge. After breakfast we set out; and this time I took Ernest as well as Fritz, as we should need all available workers.

To Ernest our expedition afforded the highest delight. We rowed till we reached the current from the river, which soon sent us on beyond the bay; but scarcely had we passed a little islet, lying to one side of us, than we saw a number of sea-gulls and other birds, so we steered for the spot to see what drew them together.

Fritz, for his part, did not for a moment take his eyes from the islet where the birds were. Suddenly he exclaimed:

'I see what it is; the birds are all pecking at a huge dead fish.'

We approached near enough to land, and after anchoring the boat with a stone, we stole softly up to the birds. So eagerly were they occupied with their feast that not one of them attempted to fly off and we might have killed great numbers of them with our sticks alone. Fritz did not cease to express his wonder at the size of the fish they were attacking, and asked me how it could have got there ?

'I believe,' I answered, 'you were yourself the means; it is probably the very shark you wounded yesterday.'

'Yes, yes, it is the very same,' he said joyously, 'I see the marks of the shot in his head.'

'It is hideous enough,' continued I, 'even when dead it makes one shudder. See what a huge mouth he has, and what a rough and prickly skin; and his length must be above twenty feet. Let us take away with us some pieces of his skin, for it may be useful to us.'

Ernest drew out the iron ramrod from his gun, and by striking with it to right and left among the birds, soon dispersed them. Fritz and I then cut several long strips of the skin from the head of the shark; these we carried to our boat, but on the way I noticed some planks and timbers which had recently been cast by the sea on this little island. On measuring the longest we found that they would answer our purpose; and after some difficulty we got them into the boat, and thus spared ourselves the trouble of going on to the ship. Some of them we tied together like a raft, and this we fastened to the end of the boat, so that we were ready to return in four hours from the time we had started, and had done a good day's work. I accordingly pushed again for the current, which drove us out to sea; then I tacked about, and resumed the direct route for the bay. All this succeeded well. I unfurled my sail, and a brisk wind soon sent us to our landing-place.

While we were sailing Fritz nailed the strips of skin we had cut from the shark to the mast to dry, and he presently noticed that they had taken a curve in drying as when they were still on the shark, and could not be made flat again.

'That was what I wanted,' I replied; 'they will be more useful to us round than flat; you know perhaps that it will be a kind of shagreen leather, if we can rub off the sharp points and afterwards polish it.'

'I thought,' said Ernest, 'that shagreen was made of ass's skin.'

'That is correct,' I said, 'but very good shagreen is also made from the skin of sea-fish, particularly in France.'

Ernest asked his brother if he knew why the mouth of the shark is not, as in other animals, placed in the middle of the snout, but directly under. Fritz confessed ignorance.

'I suppose,' Ernest went on, 'that mouth of the shark is thus placed to prevent him from depopulating the sea. With such a voracious appetite nothing would escape him if he could seize his prey without turning his body; but as it is, there is time for a smaller animal to make his escape.'

'Well reasoned,' cried I; for though Ernest's conceit sometimes made him didactic, yet I knew he had a genuine interest in natural history, and did not wish to discourage him.

We once more landed safely on shore, but no one of the family appeared. We called to them, however, and were answered, and in a few minutes my wife appeared between the two little boys. Each carried a handkerchief, which appeared filled with some new prize; and little Francis had a small fishing-net formed like a bag and strung upon a stick, which he carried on his shoulder. No sooner did they hear our voices than they hurried to meet us, surprised at our quick return. Jack reached us first, and opening the handkerchief he held, he poured out some lobsters at our feet; his mother and little Francis produced each as many more, and all alive, so that we were sure of excellent dinners for some days at least. Some of the lobsters began scuttling away in different directions, and the boys were kept in full chase, sometimes pleased and sometimes angry, sometimes laughing, sometimes scolding, for no sooner had they seized on one than ten more had followed his example.

'Isn't it lovely, papa?' said little Francis. 'I found them. Look, there are more than two hundred of them; and see how large they are, and what fine claws they have!'

'Excellent,' I said, 'and these lobsters are of a different kind from that which nipped Jack, and will make much better eating. Tell me all about it.'

'I'll tell you,' cried Jack. 'Francis and I were down by the river, when he suddenly saw the dead jackal, we threw away yesterday, all covered with lobsters; and legions more were coming in with the stream. I ran to tell mamma, who quickly got the net, and partly with that and partly with our hands, we caught numbers in a very few minutes, and we should have caught more if we had not heard you call, for the river is quite full of them.'

'You took enough for once, my boy,' said I, 'and I'm sure we shall all enjoy them.'

After we had discussed the subject a little further, my wife went back to the fire to begin cooking, and Fritz and I untied the raft of timbers and planks, and drew it inland. I then imitated the example of the Laplanders, in harnessing reindeer to their sledges. I put a piece of rope, with a running knot at the end, round the neck of the donkey, and passed the other end between its legs; to this rope I tied a piece of wood. The cow was harnessed in the same manner, and thus we made the animals pull all the timber bit by bit to the spot we had chosen for the bridge. It was a place where the shore on each side was steep, and of equal height; there was also an old trunk of a tree lying on the ground, which I foresaw would have its use.

'Now then, boys,' said I, 'the first thing is to see if our timbers are long enough to reach to the other side; measuring by my eye, I should think they are.'

'Let us tie a stone to the end of a ball of string, and throw it across,' suggested Ernest. 'Then we shall know exactly.'

It was a good thought, and answered admirably. By this method we found that the distance from one side to the other was eighteen feet. Allowing three feet more for the part of the planks that was to rest on each bank, I reckoned we ought to have planks twenty-four feet long, and I found that many we had brought were about this length.

There now remained the difficulty of carrying one end across the stream; but we determined to discuss this while we had lunch, which had been waiting for us more than an hour.

We therefore turned homewards and found that my wife had prepared for us a large dish of lobsters; but before beginning she insisted we should look at something she had made. It was two sacks intended for the donkey; these she had sewed together with thread, so that they

34

might act as panniers or bags to hang on both sides of his back. I was very glad to see them as they would be most useful in transporting our household stuff when we moved.

We hurried through our meal, being deeply interested in the work we were about to undertake, and the minute we had done hastened back to the scene of our labours.

The first thing I did towards the building of the bridge was to fasten one of the planks to the trunk of the tree, of which I have already spoken, by a strong cord; I then fastened a second cord to the other end of the plank, and tying a stone to it flung it to the opposite bank. I next crossed the river, taking with me a pulley, which I tied to a tree; I passed my second cord, that which had the stone fastened to it, through the pulley, and recrossing the river with this cord in my hand, I harnessed the ass and cow to the end of it, then drove the animals from the bank of the river. As they moved away the cord ran through the pulley on the further river bank and drew across the water the end of the plank attached to it. Presently, to my great joy, I saw it touch the other side. In a moment Fritz and Jack leaped upon it and crossed the stream upon this narrow but effective bridge.

The first timber being thus laid, a second and a third were fixed with the greatest ease. Fritz and I, standing on opposite sides of the river, placed them at such distances from each other as was necessary to form a broad and handsome bridge; what now remained to be done was to lay some short planks across them quite close to each other, which we did so quickly that the bridge was finished in a much shorter time than I should have thought possible.

Our work, however, had really been very hard, and we were very tired, so that, as the evening was beginning to set in, we returned to our camp, where we ate an excellent supper, and went to bed.

CHAPTER VIII

WE MOVE TO THE FOREST

As soon as we were up and had breakfasted the next morning, I directed my sons to gather together our whole flock of animals, and to leave the ass and the cow to me, that I might load them with the sacks. I had filled these, putting in them all the things we should stand most in need of for the two or three first days — working implements, kitchen utensils, the captain's service of plate, and a small provision of butter. I afterwards added our hammocks, and we were about to start when my wife said:

'We must not leave our fowls behind, for fear that the jackals should eat them. We must find a place for them among the luggage, and also one for little Francis, who cannot walk so far. Then there is my enchanted bag,' she added, smiling, 'which must not be left behind; for who can tell what may yet pop out of it?'

I therefore placed the child on the ass's back, fixing the enchanted bag in such a way as to support him.

In the meanwhile the other boys had been running after the cocks and hens and pigeons, but had not succeeded in catching one of them. Their mother laughed at them, and, stepping into the tent, brought out two handfuls of corn, which she scattered. The fowls came at once to pick them up. She then walked slowly before them, dropping the grain all the way, till they had followed her into the tent. When she saw them all inside, busily employed in picking up the grain, she shut the entrance, and caught one after the other without difficulty. The fowls were tied by the feet and wings, put into a basket covered with a net, and placed in triumph on the top of our luggage.

We had packed and put in the tent everything we meant to leave, and for greater security fastened down the ends of the sail-cloth at the entrance by driving stakes through them into the ground. Then at last we set out, each of us, great and small, carrying a gun upon his shoulder and a game-bag at his back. My wife led the way with her eldest son, the cow and the ass followed immediately behind them; the goat, conducted by Jack, came next, with the little monkey seated on his back, making grimaces; after this came Ernest, driving the sheep; while I brought up the rear, and the dogs ran up and down. Our march was slow, and there was something solemn and patriarchal about it; I fancied we were like our forefathers journeying in the desert, accompanied by their families and their possessions.

When we had advanced half-way across the bridge the sow thought she would come too. At the moment of our departure she had shown herself so restive that we had been compelled to leave her behind; but, seeing that we had all left the place, she set out to overtake us.

In order that our animals should not stray among the thick grass on the other side of the river I directed our march towards the seashore. But scarcely were we on the sands when our two dogs, which had strayed behind among the grass set up a howl, as if they had been attacked by some formidable animal. Fritz in an instant raised his gun ready to fire; Ernest drew back to his mother's side; Jack ran bravely after Fritz with his gun upon his shoulder; while I followed. In spite of my exhortations to proceed with caution, the boys made but three jumps to the place from whence the noise proceeded, and Jack cried out:

'Come quickly, father; here is an enormous porcupine.'

I soon reached the spot. The dogs were running to and fro with bleeding noses, and when they went too near the animal he made a noise, and darted his quills so suddenly at them that a number stuck into their coats, and made them howl violently.

While we were looking on, Jack took one of the pistols which he carried in his belt, and fired it at the head of the porcupine, so that he fell dead. This success raised Jack to the height of joy and vanity, while Fritz was so jealous he almost shed tears.

'Is it right, Jack,' he said, 'that such a little boy as you should fire like that?'

Jack only laughed.

'Pop — dead as a herring!' cried he gleefully. 'Don't you wish you had done it?'

'Come, come, boys,' said I, 'no envious speeches and no reproaches; luck for one to-day, for another tomorrow; but all for the common good.'

We now all examined the porcupine, which was an extraordinary animal. The boys tried to take hold of it, but the quills pricked their hands, and made them grimace. After some difficulty, however, we wrapped it up in a piece of sail-cloth and slung it on to the back of the donkey behind Francis, for I knew that porcupine's flesh was good to eat, and so I did not like to waste so much valuable meat. A rather ludicrous incident occurred, however, when the donkey felt the prick of the spines through the wrappings; he flung up his heels, and would have dashed off had not Fritz caught him. We thereupon readjusted the bundle so that it should not hurt him, and reassured Francis, who was a little frightened at the unexpected friskiness of his steed. After this incident we at length formed our procession again, and marched on to the giant trees. These were indeed astonishing to me, who had not seen them before, and I gratified my wife by my loudly-expressed admiration of her cleverness in judging how delightful a residence they would make.

We first released our animals from their burdens and tied their forelegs loosely together with a cord, that they might not go far away. We then let out the cocks and hens from their basket, and settled down to discuss how we could best pass the night.

Meantime Fritz, who was longing to distinguish himself as Jack had done, had slipped away, and we now heard a shot, and a few minutes later saw him running towardss us, holding a dead animal of uncommon beauty by the paws.

'Father, father, look, here is a tiger-cat,' said he, proudly raising it in the air to show it to the best advantage.

I congratulated him on having rid the world of a beast that would have made short work of our fowls.

'I saw it creeping along a branch,' he said, 'and fired at it; it fell to the ground furious and snarling, then I finished it off with another shot.'

'You were lucky to get off so easily,' I said. 'I recognise the creature very well — it is a kind of wild cat called the margay, and though it is so small, it is very savage, and might easily have wounded you dangerously.'

'Its eyes glared fiercely,' he remarked. 'Look at its lovely skin, all black and gold! May I make a belt of it?'

I agreed readily, and after this I had no peace until I had shown him how to flay the animal in the best way, which I did by hanging up the porcupine to the bough of a tree and skinning it, while Fritz watched me intently, and afterwards applied the same method to his wild cat. I then cut off part of the flesh of the porcupine to be roasted and set aside the remainder to be smoked or salted for future use.

Presently little Francis came running up to us, with his mouth crammed full of something, and called out: 'Mamma, I have found a nice fruit to eat, and I have brought you some of it!'

'You greedy boy !' replied his mother, quite alarmed, 'What have you got there? Do not put into your mouth everything you find or you will be poisoned.' She made him open his mouth, and with some difficulty drew out the remains of a fig.

'A fig!' I exclaimed. 'Where did you get it?'

'I got it among the grass, papa; and there are a great many more. I thought it must be good to eat, for the fowls and the pigeons, and even the pig, ate up all they could find.'

'We are, then, in a grove of fig-trees,' I said. 'Not the dwarf figs we see in Europe, but a kind called yellow mangoes, which I know do send down their branches to take root in just this peculiar way.'

38

I took this opportunity to tell the boys never to eat anything they found till they had seen it eaten by birds and monkeys. At the word monkeys they turned to look at our little monkey, who was sitting on the root of a tree, examining with the oddest grimaces the half-skinned tiger-cat which lay near him. Francis offered him a fig, which he first turned round and round, then smelt, and finally ate with pleasure.

'Bravo Mr Monkey!' exclaimed the boys, clapping their hands.

My wife had made a fire by this time, and put on the pot to prepare our dinner. The tiger-cat was given to the dogs, who tore it to pieces. While our dinner was being made ready, I employed my time in making packing-needles with some of the quills of the porcupine, which I had pulled out. I heated a large nail red-hot; then pierced the thick end of the quills with it, and soon had presented my wife with a large packet of long, stout needles, which she was delighted with, as she meant to make some better harness for our animals. I recommended her to be careful in the use of her packthread, for I saw we should want it to make a ladder for ascending the tree when we began to live there.

For this purpose I had chosen the highest fig-tree; and while we were waiting for dinner I made the boys try how high they could throw a stick or stone into it. I also tried myself; but the lowest branches were so far from the ground that none of us could touch them. I saw, therefore, that we must think of some idea for fastening the end of the ladder to them. Then Fritz asked me how he could clean his new margay skin, and I showed him how to spread it out in the bed of the stream, under running water, fixed down by large stones. After this we returned, and dined heartily on some slices of ham and bread and cheese, under the shade of our beautiful trees.

While we ate I was considering the difficulty of getting up the tree, and at last I saw that we should be obliged to pass the night on the ground. So we began to sling our hammocks to some of the arched roots of the trees, spreading over them a piece of sail-cloth large enough to cover them, to keep off the dew and the insects. I then went with the two eldest boys to the seashore, to choose some pieces of wood to make steps for the ladder. Ernest discovered in a sort of bog some bamboo canes, which were just the thing. I cut them with my hatchet in pieces of four or five feet long, and the boys bound them together to carry back. At the same time I chose some of the straightest and most slender of the stalks, with which to make arrows, in case we might want them.

Seeing that the bamboos grew more thickly a little way off, I went towardss them, when suddenly Flora, who had come with us, made several jumps, and threw herself furiously into the middle of the bushes; at the same moment a flock of flamingoes sprang out, and mounted into the air. Fritz fired, and two of the birds fell. One of them was quite dead; the other was only slightly wounded in the wing, and ran so fast towardss the water that we were afraid he would escape us. Fritz plunged after him, up to his knees in the water; and Flora, coming to his help, caught hold of the flamingo and held him by the wing, though the bird struggled and flapped violently. When he had been dragged out we found some difficulty in securing him, though I tied his feet with my handkerchief, and held him under my left arm.

The boys were delighted to have captured such a fine bird alive, and spoke of being able to tame him.

'He is a bird to be easily tamed,' I said, 'for he is of a tractable though timid disposition.'

'We will catch some little fish for him,' said Ernest, who knew something of the habits of these birds. Then he examined the prize more attentively. 'What long legs he has!' he added. 'Are all flamingoes like this — of such a beautiful red colour, with wings tinted with purple? I think I have seen the flamingo in my Natural History, and the colours were not like these.'

'I believe that the plumage is differently coloured according to the age of the birds,' I told him. 'When very young they are grey; then they turn white; and it is only when they are full grown that they are adorned with this beautiful tinted plumage.'

Talking like this, we returned to our camp laden with bundles of canes of various sizes, and with the dead and living birds. We were greeted with the delight that a new discovery never failed to bring; only my wife, with her usual anxiety about ways and means, asked where we should get food enough for all the new animals we brought home?

I told her I expected this acquisition would soon be able to feed himself; and I proceeded to examine his wound. I found that only one wing was injured by the shot, but that the other had also been slightly hurt by the dog laying hold of him. I rubbed some ointment on both, and this seemed to relieve him. I next tied him by one of his legs with a long string to a stake I had driven into the ground quite near to the river, that he might go in and wash himself when he liked.

Now I had begun to think seriously of the difficulty of getting a rope ladder to reach even the lowest of the branches, for the nearest to the ground were at a height of forty feet, and it would be necessary to carry a rope over these before we could fix it. I had an idea, however, and, sitting down on the grass, I began to make some arrows with the slenderest pieces of the bamboo that I had so carefully chosen. As the arrows were hollow, I filled them with the moist sand to give them a little weight; and, lastly, I tipped them with a bit of feather from the flamingo, to make them fly straight.

The boys watched me with interest, and soon saw what I was doing. Laying the arrows aside for a moment, I chose a flexible rod for a bow, and making a niche at each end, soon fixed a piece of string to draw it into a curve. Then I asked my wife if she had such a thing as a ball of string, which would unravel as I required it. She produced this with a laugh from what she called her enchanted bag. I tied the end of the ball of string to an arrow, and fixing it to the bow, I shot it off so as to make the arrow pass over one of the largest branches of the tree, and fall again to the ground; thus I had overcome the first difficulty. It was now easy to tie a piece of rope to the end of the string, and draw it upwards, till the knot reached the same branch. Then I knew that, when the ladder was finished, we should at any rate be able to pull it up to the bough.

So I turned my attention to the ladder itself, a much more difficult job. The first thing was to cut a length of about one hundred feet from our stock of ropes; this I divided into two equal pieces, which I laid on the ground at the distance of a foot from each other. I told Fritz to cut the canes we had brought in pieces each two feet in length. As he did this, Ernest handed them to me one after another; and I inserted them into my ropes at the distance of twelve inches apart, fixing them with knots in the rope. Jack, at the same time, by my order, drove into each a long nail at both ends to prevent their slipping out again. Thus, in a very short time, we had made a ladder of forty steps, firm and compact, which we all regarded with joyful surprise. I now tied it with strong knots to the end of the rope which hung from the tree, and pulled it up till it reached the branch, and rested so well upon it, that the exclamations of the boys resounded from all sides. Everyone wished to be the first to ascend, but I decided that it should be Jack, he being the nimblest and the lightest among them. Accordingly, I and his brothers held the ends of the rope, and of the ladder, as well as we could, while he ran easily up, and reached the branch without an accident; but, when he got there, I saw that he had not strength enough to tie the ladder firmly to the tree. So I sent Fritz up after him, not without some little anxiety, as he was much heavier than his brother. But it was not long before we saw him side by side with Jack, forty feet above our heads.

Fritz set to work to fasten the ladder by passing the rope round and round the branch, and this he did with so much sense, that I felt I might ascend myself in safety. But first I tied a large pulley to the end of the rope, and took it up with me. When I was at the top, I fastened the pulley to a branch, so that I might be able the next day to draw up the planks and timbers for building the platform of our hut. All this took so long that it was finished by the light of the moon.

For the last few minutes I had been alone on the branch, and concluded that Jack and Fritz had descended, when I suddenly heard their voices singing an evening hymn which seemed to come from the clouds. I soon gathered that instead of going down, they had gone up, and had climbed upwards from branch to branch, till they had reached the very top. I called out to them to take great care in coming down, for it was almost night, and the light of the moon scarcely penetrated the thick foliage. They soon appeared without any accident, and then I told them to gather together all our animals, and to get what dry wood we should want for making fires, which we must keep up through the night as a precaution against the attacks of wild beasts.

My wife now showed me the work she had been busy with throughout the day; some harness for the cow and the ass. Then we had our supper, while all the animals stood round us. My wife threw some grain to the fowls, and afterwards the pigeons flew up to the top of the giant tree, while the cocks and hens perched, cackling all the time, upon the rounds of the ladder. The cow and donkey we tied to the arched roots of the tree, quite near to our hammocks. Our beautiful flamingo was not forgotten. Fritz fed him with some crumbs of biscuit soaked in milk, and afterwards, putting his head under his right wing, and tucking up one leg, he went quietly to sleep, too ignorant of the ways of human beings to have any dread of them. Before retiring I made up the brushwood the boys had gathered into heaps and set fire to several of them, and then threw myself contentedly upon my hammock. The lads were already in theirs, but we soon heard them grumbling at being obliged to lie so close to each other. I called out mockingly, that they were much better off than many sailors, and that unless beds dropped from the clouds, they must put up with it; whereupon they ceased, and being really tired by their long day in the open air, they were soon asleep.

42

CHAPTER IX

OUR HOUSE IN THE GIANT TREE

AS for myself, I had quite decided that I would not go to sleep during this first night in the forest, but without telling anyone would keep watch. Every leaf that stirred gave me a thrill, making me think that a tiger, or other ferocious beast, might be creeping up to attack us. As soon as one of the bonfires was consumed, I got up quietly and lighted another; but at length finding that no animal appeared, I became reassured and fell into a sound sleep.

The next morning, after breakfast, we all eagerly set to work. My wife went off with Ernest, Jack, and Francis, leading the donkey to the seashore to collect more wood. In their absence I ascended the tree with Fritz. I found that to place such a platform as I intended would be a work of no great difficulty, for the branches grew close to each other, and on the same level. Some I cut off either with a saw or hatchet, leaving none but those that would be useful as a foundation for the floor. Above these, at the height of forty-six feet, there were others upon which we could hang our hammocks; and higher still, there was a further set of branches, admirable for supporting the roof of the hut, which at present could be formed of nothing more than a large piece of sail-cloth.

At first our work did not progress very fast. It was necessary to raise certain heavy planks to this height of forty feet. However, I fixed the pulley. and Fritz and I managed to draw them up to the branches one by one. When I had placed two of them upon the branches, I fixed the other planks upon them. I then built up a sort of wall of wood like a park-paling, all round, for safety. These operations, and a third journey to the seashore to collect more wood, filled our morning so completely, that not one of us had thought about eating. For this once we contented ourselves with a bit of ham and some milk as a light lunch; and then returned to finish our aerial palace, which began to look quite interesting. We unhooked our hammocks from their positions, and hoisted them up into the tree. The sail-cloth roof was supported by the thick branches above, and hung down on every side; so the idea occurred to me of nailing it to the paling, thus getting not only a roof, but two walls also. The immense trunk of the tree formed a third side, while in the fourth was the entrance to our hut; through which we could see what was outside, including the shore and the waves. The hammocks were soon hung on the branches, and after a hard after-noon's work we saw that we should be able to sleep in our new hut. When this was finished there was still a little daylight left, and notic-ing that all the planks had not been used, I suggested to Fritz, who had been a most hard-working and painstaking assistant all day, that we should make a table on which we could place our meals. It was not much of a table, I must confess, for we were both tired, but still, it was better than nothing, and when our supper was spread upon it by the roots of the great tree, it looked very nice. The three youngest boys had meantime collected all the pieces of wood we had thrown down from the tree, and a quantity of small twigs to form a supply for a fire.

Exhausted by the work of the day, I threw myself on the grass, and my wife having seated herself near me, I reminded her that the next day was Sunday, and suggested that as we had food to eat, and a roof to shelter us, we should spend it as a holy day.

She quite agreed, and having told the boys, we sat down near the table for supper. My wife took from the fire an earthen pot, and, raising the cover, she drew out of it, with a fork, the flamingo which Fritz had killed. She told us that she had preferred cooking it in this way to roasting it, because Ernest had said it was an old bird, which would be better stewed. We chaffed our greedy boy a little at this, and his brothers gave him the name of the *cook*. However, we felt obliged to him all the same, for the bird was excellent, and was eaten up to the very bones.

While we were enjoying it, the live flamingo stalked up to the place where we were sitting. He was so tame that we had released him from the stake. His fine plumage was most beautiful. He took his walks gravely from place to place, and looked seriously on life; while, on the other hand, the tricks and the grimaces of our monkey amused us much. The little animal had become quite familiar with us; jumped from shoulder to shoulder; always caught adroitly what we threw to him, and ate it so eagerly that we laughed heartily.

The boys now lighted one of the heaps of wood.Then we tied long ropes loosely round the necks of our dogs, meaning to take the ends up the ladder with us, so as to prevent them from straying away. Every one was eager to climb to the new hut, and the three eldest boys ran up like monkeys; then came their mother's turn; she took a little time, being rather uncomfortable on the thin swaying ladder, but she arrived safely.

My own turn was last, and most difficult, for I carried little Francis on my back; and as I had released the foot of the ladder so that I might draw it up after me, it swung backwards and forwards more than ever.

44

At last, however, I arrived at the top, and drew the ladder up too. It seemed to the boys as if we were in one of the strong castles of old times, in which, when the drawbridge was raised, no enemy could get in. Notwithstanding, I kept the guns in readiness.

I was so tired with all I had done that I fell asleep almost instantly, and we all slept so soundly that it was broad daylight before any of us were awake.

We were so accustomed to lovely weather here in this beautiful climate that it was no surprise to us to find, when we waked from a sound and refreshing sleep, that another glorious day dawned upon us. After breakfast we all drew together beneath the trees, which, with the wide-spreading branches, made a semblance of a cathedral aisle, and I held a short service.

I could remember enough of the Church Service to go through it tolerably well, and as the boys knew several Psalms by heart, our service was fairly complete.

The only thing I lacked was a Bible, and when I mentioned this my wife produced one from her 'enchanted bag' and gravely handed it to me. Having read a few chapters I then, by way of a sermon, told the boys an allegory I had made up for them, and afterwards listened with pleasure to the questions and comments on it.

When the service was finished, and we had had our midday meal, I made no objection to the boys wandering off to amuse themselves as they liked best, knowing that the day was one for innocent recreation, after due attention had been given to things of the spirit. I only stipulated that no firearms should be used, as we had sufficient food, and any form of taking life without necessity was to be avoided. As we were all thoroughly tired with the hard work of the preceeding week, however, not one of the party went very far, and the rest of the day passed peacefully without accident of any kind.

It had occurred to me that our supply of ammunition for the guns was not inexhaustible, and that there might come a time when we should have to rely chiefly on bows and arrows for our hunting. It was well, therefore, to get all the practice with these weapons that we could. So the next morning I set to work to make another bow, meaning to teach the boys to use it when it should be ready.

I spent most of the day in shaping and bending new bows and in manufacturing arrows, though the work was diversified by a lesson in tanning which I gave to Fritz, when he took his wild cat's skin out of the stream where he had left it to be cleaned.

I told him how to get rid of the fat on the skin, by rubbing it over with sand; next to rub it with soft butter, to make it supple, and then to stretch it in different directions; and also to make use of some eggs if he could get them.

When he had cut off enough of the skin to make himself a belt, he said he would like to make little cases of the rest to hold a knife, fork, and spoon, so that we could carry them with us on our expeditions.

So I showed him how to cut certain small cylinders of wood of the size and length required; then to stretch the softened skin upon the surface in such a way that it reached a little beyond the wood, then when it dried it would fit to the wood and stick to it tightly.

He was doing this when we heard the firing of a gun, which seemed to come from our tent in the tree, and several birds at the same time fell dead at our feet. Looking up, we saw Ernest standing outside the tent, with a gun in his hand, and heard him triumphantly exclaiming:

'Catch them! I have hit them.'

He climbed down joyfully, and ran with Francis to pick up the fallen birds, while Fritz and Jack instantly rushed up the ladder to try to shoot birds too.

One of the dead birds was a sort of thrush, and the others were a very small kind of pigeon, which in the Antilles is called an ortolan, very fat, and of a delicious taste. We noticed that these birds were attracted by the wild figs, which were ripening. I gave the boys leave to kill as many as they liked. I knew that, half roasted and put into barrels with melted butter thrown over them, they would keep for a long time, and might prove an excellent resource. My wife set about stripping off the feathers of the birds to cook them for our dinner. I sat by her and went on with my work of arrow-making.

The ortolans, which we ate at dinner-time, were certainly excellent, but there were hardly enough to go round, and there was not much on them. However, we comforted ourselves by the thought that we had an inexhaustible store to draw upon if we were skilful enough to hit them.

CHAPTER X

PRICKLY FIGS AND POTATOES

WHILE we were eating I suggested to the boys that we should name the different places on our island, so that we could refer to them in conversation.

They all agreed joyfully, and Ernest at once began reciting the very longest names he could think of, such as *Monomotaqua*, *Zanzibar*, *Coromandel*, and many others.

I laughed at him, and pointed out we should only give ourselves unnecessary trouble by acting so foolishly, and proposed we should christen the places according to something which had happened to ourselves there. For instance, we might call the bay where we landed Deliverance Bay.

'Oh no,' cried Jack; 'let it be called Lobster Bay, after the beast who caught hold of my leg.'

'We might call it Weeping Bay,' suggested Fritz mischievously 'in memory of the tears you shed there.'

I interposed to prevent Jack's quick retort, and we all agreed on Deliverance Bay. We went on to call the place where we had lived the first few days Tent House, and the island on which the shark had died Shark Island.

Then followed Flamingo Marsh and Jackal River, and finally, after rejecting such names as Tree Castle and Fig Town for our present abode, we agreed to call it Falcon's Nest.

These important points settled, Jack asked me to help him to make a sort of protective harness for the dogs from the porcupine skin, which he had cleaned in the same way as Fritz had cleaned that of the wild cat. It did not take long to fasten a shield of it over the shoulders of the dogs. Turk did not seem to object, but Flora was very angry and rolled about scrubbing herself against the trees to get rid of the encumbrance, so at last we took it off. Of the rest of the skin Jack made himself a sort of round cap which he wore with his usual air of mischievous impudence.

During the afternoon I resumed my occupation of making and shaping bows and arrows, and by Jack's suggestion, used some of the soup-cakes, slightly melted, to serve as glue, such as little Francis had imagined it to be, for fixing on the feathers to the arrow-heads.

It was very hot all the afternoon, too hot to wander from the shade, but as the evening advanced and the intense heat of the day cooled, I thought we might all go off on an expedition of some kind.

'Let us go to Tent House, father,' said Fritz, 'we are in want of powder and shot for the ortolans.'

'I too vote for Tent House,' said my wife, 'my butter is nearly gone.'

'If we do go,' added Ernest, 'let us try to bring away some of the geese and ducks with us; they will look very well swimming about in our stream here by Falcon's Nest.'

'And I,' cried Francis, 'will catch a handkerchief full of lobsters in Jackal River, and we will put them into Falcon Stream'

So we set out. Fritz was adorned with his fine belt of wild-cat skin. Jack had his belt in which he carried two pistols, and wore his bristling cap of porcupine skin. Each carried a gun and a game-bag; even little Francis had a bow which I had given him, and a quiver on his shoulder. Their mother carried the large butter-pot, to fill it from the storehouse. Turk marched before us with his coat of porcupine spines.

Our way along the stream was at first extremely pleasant, being sheltered by the shade of large trees, while the ground under our feet was covered with a short and soft kind of grass.

The eldest boys ran on or made expeditions this way and that, foraging. Presently they hurried back full gallop, and this time, for a wonder, grave Ernest was first. He reached me panting for breath, and so full of joy and eagerness, that he could not pronounce a word distinctly, but he held out his hand, which contained three little balls of a light green colour.

'We have found a prize indeed, father,' he cried, when he had recovered his voice; 'we have found some potatoes.'

'What, potatoes!' I exclaimed, for I scarcely dared believe in such good luck. 'This is indeed a discovery.'

We all rushed to the place where the potatoes had been found, and saw there a number of potato plants, many of them covered with lilac and yellow flowers, more delightful to us than if they had been fragrant roses. Jack bawled out, jumping for joy: 'They are really potatoes, and though I did not discover them, at least I will dig them up.'

Saying this, he knelt down and began to scratch them up from the earth with his hands; the rest of us set to work also, and with our knives and sticks we soon rooted out enough to fill our bags and our pockets.

This happy discovery delayed us a little, but at last we continued our journey. Ernest's discovery of the potatoes was not to be the only one that day, however.

All the way I had noted different kinds of grasses, many of them of the thorn-leaved species, and stronger than those cultivated in the greenhouses of Europe. There were also in abundance the Indian fig, with its large broad leaf; aloes of different forms and colours; the superb prickly candle, or cactus, bearing straight stalks, taller than a man, and crowned with long straight branches, forming a sort of star. The broad plantain spread along the rock, its innumerable twisted boughs hanging down perpendicularly, and ornamented with flowers, which grew in large tufts, and were of the brightest rose-colour; but that which pleased us best, and which we found in great abundance, was the king of fruits, the pine-apple, which we all feasted on with delight.

Soon after, I discovered among the multitude of plants, which grew either at the foot or in the clefts of the rock, the karata, many plants of which were now in blossom. I pointed out to the boys the immense size of its leaves, hollowed in the middle like saucers, so that they hold the rain for a long time, also its beautiful red flowers. I knew that the pith of this plant is used as tinder by the negroes, who also make a strong kind of thread from the fibres of its leaves. Wishing to show how useful it was, I asked Ernest to take out my flint and steel.

Then breaking off a dried stalk of the plant, I stripped off the bark, and showed inside a kind of dry spongy substance, which I laid upon the flint; on striking it with steel, it instantly caught fire. The boys looked on with astonishment, and soon exclaimed:

'We'll call it the fire-tree!'

But this was not all. On turning up the leaves I showed some red fibres, which could be pulled off and were as strong as thread. Of course, they were not long, being only the length of the leaf itself, but none the less they would be very valuable.

It was difficult to detach them owing to the prickles which grew thickly round them, but I knew that if we put the leaves to dry, either in the sun or by a gentle fire, the useless part of the leaf would separate after being beaten, and the mass of thread would remain.

My wife exclaimed with pleasure at this, having been anxious as to how she could renew her stock of thread when it was exhausted, and she remarked to her boys how useful a thing it was to read and remember, otherwise we should never have known of the supply of good things by which we were surrounded.

The next plant I noticed was the Indian fig, or prickly pear, which grew upon the rocks, and seemed to flourish the better the poorer the soil.

There was growing on it a kind of fig, and I showed the boys how to gather this prickly fruit without hurting their fingers. As the figs were growing at a considerable height, I threw up a stone and brought one down, which I caught upon my hat; I cut off one end and held it on a knife while I peeled off the skin, and then gave it to the others to taste. They liked it, and very soon got some for themselves. I saw Ernest holding one upon the end of his knife, turning it about in all directions and looking at it curiously.

'I wish I could know,' he said at length, 'what little animals these are in the fig, they are bright scarlet.'

'Let me look,' I said; 'I believe that it is the insect called the cochineal, which is used in dyeing, for nothing else produces so fine a scarlet. In America they stretch cloths under the branches and shake the tree, and when the insects have fallen in great numbers they are sprinkled with vinegar or cold water, and then dried and sent to Europe.'

I explained to the boys, also, that the thorny stalks of the prickly pear are often used to form stockades, which are particularly effective because made with so little trouble, for if you plant only one of the leaves in the ground it immediately takes root, and grows with astonishing rapidity.

Jack, the thoughtless, here began to cut down with his clasp-knife a pretty large plant, striking to right and left with all his might, to show that he would not be daunted by such a fence, when one of the divided leaves fell with such violence against his leg that the thorns struck into the flesh, and he roared out piteously. We could not help laughing at him, and congratulating him on the success of his demonstration.

Ernest was anxious that we should there and then make a thorn hedge around our banyan tree, but I told him this would come all in good time.

We now left the beautiful strip of forest, rich in many plants which are only to be found in Europe in greenhouses and conservatories, and made our way through the tall grass to Jackal River, which we crossed by Family Bridge.

Soon after we arrived at Tent House, where we found everything as we had left it. Fritz loaded himself with powder and shot; I and my wife and Francis employed ourselves in filling the pot with butter; Ernest and Jack looked about for the geese and ducks, but could not succeed in catching one of them. Ernest then took a small bit of cheese, and, tying it to the end of a piece of string, he held it floating in the water. When the birds swallowed it, he drew them gently towards him one by one till he had caught them all, while we watched, amused at his ingenuity.

We had meant to take back some salt, but as the sacks were filled with potatoes, we could only throw a little into one of them.

We then set out loaded on our return. The ducks and geese, being packed in cloths and tied on our backs with only their heads and necks out, looked very odd, and we could not help laughing at each other.

The laughter seemed to make the walk back shorter, and we were soon again seated under our tree at Falcon Stream. My wife at once put some of the potatoes on the fire. She next milked the cow and goats, and gave us each some milk to drink, which we were glad of, as the walk had made us thirsty.

When the potatoes were at last cooked they turned out excellent, and we made a hearty supper on them before climbing our ladder to rest in our aerial castle.

CHAPTER XI

ERNEST SHOOTS A KANGAROO

I HAD noticed on the shore many pieces of wood, of which I thought I could make a kind of sledge, so that we could drag our cask of butter and other provisions from Tent House to Falcon Stream, and so save ourselves the labour of future journeys.

I woke early next morning, meaning to set to work before the others were awake and I roused Ernest to help me, thinking it better to leave Fritz with the family, as he was the tallest and strongest. Ernest got up willingly enough, and we descended the ladder without disturbing the others. We harnessed the donkey, and I made him draw some large branches of a tree which I wanted.

We were not long in finding the pieces of wood, and set to work to cut them the proper length, and then we laid them crossways on the branches, which made for them a sledge of a sort. We added to the load a little chest, which we found half buried in the sands, quite close to the waves, and then we set out on our return to Falcon Stream. We found the others up, and interested to hear where we had been. The chest we had brought was soon opened by a strong hatchet, for all were eager to see what was inside. It contained, however, only some sailors' clothes and some linen, which were wet with the sea.

We then sat down to breakfast, and afterwards Fritz and Jack showed me no less than fifty dead ortolans and thrushes. I found that they had used so large a quantity of powder and shot in this sport that I stopped them, and taught them how to make some snares of the thread of the karata, to be hung from the branches of the fig-tree. The boys were both interested and eager, and so clever at it that Jack succeeded in his very first attempt. I left Francis with him, and took Fritz and Ernest to help me in making the sledge.

As we were hard at work a great noise was heard among the fowls; the cock crowed louder than the rest, and the hens ran to and fro cackling. We all hastened up, and Ernest, happening to look at the monkey, noticed that he jumped quickly into a hollow place under one of the roots of the tree and hid himself. Ernest was at the place as soon as he, and caught him with a new-laid egg in his paw, which he was going to hide. The monkey sprang away to another hole, and Ernest followed; here also he found some eggs, and brought them in his hat to his mother. It was plain to see that the monkey had seized the eggs as soon as the hens had laid them. We inflicted no other punishment upon him for this naughtiness than that of tying him up when the hens were about to lay.

In the meanwhile Jack had got up into the tree, and had arranged some of the snares in the branches; he came down again to tell us that our pigeons had made a sort of nest there of some dry grass, and that it already contained several eggs.

During these arrangements the boys and I had been busily employed, and now our work was completed, and we had made a rough kind of sledge for the donkey to draw. On looking up, when we had finished, I found that my wife had spitted the birds which the boys had killed, and was roasting them on an officer's sword which Fritz had brought from the ship. I was inclined to blame her profusion in cooking more birds at once than we could eat, but she reminded me that I had myself advised her to half-roast the birds before putting them into butter, to be preserved for future use. She said also that, as I had now a sledge, I might go to Tent House after dinner to fetch the cask of butter. I had no objection to this, and determined to go to Tent House the same day. I decided to take Ernest with me this time, and was pleased to see that Fritz displayed no jealousy at the proposal; in fact, at the moment of departure he presented us with cases of his own workmanship, made from his wild-cat skin, which were intended to hold spoons and knives and forks, while room was left in the middle for a little hatchet. We thanked him for his gifts, which were really very well done.

We had harnessed the donkey and the cow to our sledge; we each took a piece of bamboo cane in hand to serve as a whip; and resting our guns upon our shoulders, began our journey. Flora was to come with us, and Turk to remain behind. We took the road by the seashore, for the sledge ran more easily here than in the thick wild grass. We reached Family Bridge, on Jackal River, and arrived at Tent House without adventure, and unharnessed the animals to let them graze, while we set to work to load the sledge with the cask of butter, the cask of cheese, a small barrel of gun-powder, different instruments, and some ball and shot. We were so busy that we forgot all about the animals, until, looking up suddenly, we found they had re-crossed the bridge and wandered out of sight. I told Ernest to go with Flora and bring them back, and in the meantime went to look for a place to bathe in on the other side of Tent House. In a short time I found myself at Deliverance Bay, which ended in a marsh producing some fine bul-rushes; and further on, a chain of steep rocks, jutting into the sea, formed a set of little creeks excellent for bathing. As Ernest had not returned, I amused myself with cutting some of the rushes. And when he did turn up, I told him to fill a small bag with some of the salt there was here, and then to empty it into the large one for the ass to carry. 'Meantime I will bathe, and then it will be your turn, and mine to take care of the animals,' I said.

I returned to the rocks, and enjoyed my dip, but I did not stay long, and I had just dressed myself, when I heard his voice calling out, 'Father, father, a fish! A fish of monstrous size! Run quickly; I can hardly hold him! He is eating up my line!' I ran to the place and found Ernest lying along the ground on his face, pulling in his line, to which. a large fish was attached, struggling violently. I ran hastily and snatched the rod out of his hand, for I feared the weight of the fish might pull him into the water. I played the fish, and then drew him gently along into a shallow, from which he could not escape, and thus we caught him. He was a salmon, and must have weighed not less than fifteen pounds, so that the capture was magnificent.

'You have worked hard,' I said to Ernest,' and you had better wipe the perspiration from your face, and keep quiet for a short time before you go into the water.'

'It was fortunate,' he remarked, 'that I thought of bringing my fishing-rod.'

'Certainly it was. But how did you see this large fish, and what made you think you could catch it?'

'I had noticed,' said Ernest, 'the fish about here, and that made me think of bringing the rod with me. On my way to the salt I saw a lot of little crabs near the water's edge. I thought I would try to bait my hook with one of them, but at first I caught only a dozen little fish, which are there in my handkerchief; then I saw that they were chased in the water by big fish, so I baited my hook with one of the little ones; but the hook was too small, and my rod too weak. So I took one of the finest of the bulrushes you had just gathered, and put a larger hook on my line, and in a short time the large fish there seized upon the bait. However, if you had not come I should either have let go my line, or have been dragged into the water, for he was much stronger than I.'

We now examined the smaller fish, which were mostly trout and herrings. I cut them all open, and rubbed them inside with salt that they might not go bad in the heat. While I was thus employed Ernest went to the rocks and bathed, and I had time to fill some more bags with salt before his return. We then harnessed and loaded our animals, and went back to Falcon Stream.

When we were about half-way, Flora, who was before us, suddenly sprang off, and began barking. We soon after saw her chasing an animal, which made the most extraordinary jumps. This creature passed close to where I stood. I fired, but its flight was so rapid that I did not hit it. Ernest, who was behind, hearing the report of my gun, fired the next minute, and his aim was so good that the animal fell dead. I ran to look at it. It was as large as a sheep, but the tail was like that of a tiger; its snout and hair were like those of a mouse, and its teeth were like a hare's but much larger; the fore legs resembled those of the squirrel, and were extremely short; but to make up for this, its hind legs were as long as a pair of stilts. We examined the creature a long time in silence, and I did not pronounce its name, as I wanted to see if Ernest would recognise it. For a moment he did not, and then cried out joyously:

'A kangaroo! I never thought I should see one alive!'

We spent several minutes further in examining with interest this rare animal, and then began to consider the next difficulty, which was how to get him home without spoiling his skin. We managed this at last by tying the fore legs together, and by means of two canes, we carried him with considerable trouble to the sledge, upon which he was securely fastened.

Having now nothing more to detain us, we continued our road

towards Falcon Stream, talking with great animation about the strange beast we had found.

When we arrived somewhat late, at Falcon Stream, we heard shouts from the others, and when the three boys ran to meet us it was our turn to laugh; one had on a sailor's shirt, which trailed round him like the robe of a spectre; another was buried in a pair of trousers, which were fastened round his neck, and reached to the ground; and the third had a long waistcoat, which came down to his feet, and gave him the look of an elongated sausage. They all tried to jump about, but finding this impossible, from the length of their garments, they strutted slowly to and fro. After some hearty laughing, I asked what was the cause of this masquerade. My wife told me that the three boys had been bathing, and that she had taken the opportunity to wash all their clothes; but as they had not dried so soon as she expected, the boys had become impatient, and had taken from the sailor's chest what they wanted.

'I preferred,' said she, 'that you should see them in this odd sort of a disguise, rather than quite naked, like little savages.'

It was now our turn to give an account of our journey: and we showed her, one after another, casks, bulrushes, salt, fish, and lastly, with infinite triumph, our beautiful kangaroo. In a trice it was surrounded, examined, and admired by all, and such a number of questions asked, that Ernest and I scarcely knew which to answer first. Fritz was the only one who was a little silent. I saw plainly what was passing in his mind. He was jealous of his brother, but I also saw that he was struggling manfully against so mean a passion. In a short time he had succeeded so completely that he joined frankly in our merriment. He came near the kangaroo and examined it, then, turning to his brother, he said cordially that he had had good luck, and that he must be a good shot to have killed the animal.

'But, father,' said he, 'when you go again to Tent House, or on any other excursion, it will be my turn to go with you. For here, at Falcon Stream, there is nothing new, a few thrushes and some pigeons, this is all we have from day to day.'

'I promise you certainly,' I said, 'for I know you have fought against your jealousy. You shall go with me in my very next excursion, which will probably be tomorrow, and it will be another journey to the ship.'

We made an excellent supper on our little fish, to which we added some potatoes, and afterwards I gave some salt to each of our animals, who were heartily pleased with it. Then as we were all tired we said our prayers at an early hour, mounted our ladder, and were soon asleep.

CHAPTER XII

DRAWN BY A TURTLE

I ROSE with the first crowing of the cock, and descended the ladder, intending to set about skinning the kangaroo. I found, however, that the dogs had made an onslaught on it already. Luckily, as it hung by the hind feet, it was mostly out of their reach, but they had managed to worry the head; so I gave them a good flogging to teach them to leave such things alone in future.

My wife hearing their yelps came down, and though she owned I was in the right, she patted the dogs to console them. I now set about stripping the kangaroo without injuring the skin; but I got on so slowly that the boys came about me protesting they were starved before I had finished my work. Having at last completed it, I went to the river to wash myself thoroughly, and then to the sailor's chest to change my coat.

Breakfast over, I ordered Fritz to get ready to go to Tent House, where we had left the boat.

When we were leaving we could not find Jack or Ernest anywhere, and had to go without seeing them; but on arriving at the bridge they burst upon us out of the undergrowth with loud shouts, begging to be allowed to go with us. This I could not permit for a moment, both on account of their mother's anxiety should they not return, and because she would be left without any sort of protection. To compensate them, however, for the disappointment so plainly shown on their faces, I told Fritz to give his watch to Ernest, and promised to give him another, as well as to bring one back for Jack from the ship.

I then sent the younger boys back with a message to their mother, which I had not had the courage to tell her myself — that we might be forced to pass the night on board, and not return till the evening of the next day.

We got into the boat, and gaining the current, quickly cleared Deliverance Bay, and reached the ship. When we had fastened our boat, our first care was to select fit materials to construct a raft, as Ernest had suggested.

I found a sufficient number of water-casks, and having emptied them and replaced the bungs carefully, we threw the casks overboard, after securing them with ropes, so as to keep them together: this completed, we placed a number of planks upon them to form a firm platform or deck. Thus we made a useful raft, on which we could stow thrice as much as in our boat. This laborious task had taken up the whole day; we had scarcely allowed ourselves a minute to eat even the cold meat we had brought with us.

In the evening, Fritz and I were so weary, that it would have been impossible for us to row back to land; so we lay down in the captain's cabin, on a good mattress, which made us sleep so soundly that our intention of watching in turn, for fear of accident, was forgotten, and we both slept heavily, side by side, till broad daylight opened our eyes. We rose, and actively set to work to load our raft.

We began with stripping the cabin of its doors and windows; next we secured several chests, including the carpenter's and gunner's, containing all their tools and implements. Those we could remove with levers and rollers were put entire upon the raft, and we took out of the others all that made them too heavy. One of the captain's chests was filled with costly articles which no doubt he meant to sell — to the rich planters of Port Jackson, or give to the savages. In the collection were several gold and silver watches, buckles, shirt-buttons, necklaces, rings, as well as coin. I chose the two watches — already promised — and took a purseful of coin as a toy for Francis; but it amused me to consider of how little value these things were in our present position. The discovery that delighted me most was a chest containing some dozens of young plants of every species of European fruits, which had been carefully packed in moss for transportation. I found pear, plum, almond, peach, apple, apricot, chestnut trees, and vine shoots. In another place were bars of iron, and large pigs of lead, grinding-stones, cart-wheels ready for mounting, a complete set of farrier's instruments, tongs, shovels, plough-shares, rolls of iron and copper wire, sacks full of maize, peas, oats, vetches, and even a little hand-mill. The ship had been freighted with everything likely to be useful in a distant colony. We found a saw-mill, in separate parts, but each piece numbered, and so accurately fitted that it would be quite easy to put it together for use.

I had now to consider which of all these treasures I should take or

57

leave. It was impossible to carry with us in one trip such a mass of things, and yet we could not bring ourselves to leave them in the ship.

With difficulty and hard labour we made our choice and finished our loading, having added a large fishing-net, quite new, and the ship's great compass. With the net, Fritz found two harpoons and a rope-windlass, such as they use in the whale fishery. He asked me to let him place the harpoons, tied to the end of the rope, over the bow of our tub-boat, and I assented.

At last we stepped into the tub-boat, and with some difficulty we pushed out for the current, drawing our raft triumphantly after us with a stout rope, which we had fastened securely to its head.

The wind was favourable, and briskly swelled our sail. The sea was calm, and we advanced at a considerable rate. Fritz had for some time fixed his eyes on something of a large size which was floating on the water, and he now asked me to take the telescope and see what it could be. I soon discovered that it was a turtle, which had fallen asleep in the sun on the surface of the water. No sooner had Fritz learned this, than he begged me to steer softly to get near to it. I readily consented; but as his back was towards me, and the sail between us, I did not see what he was doing, till a violent jerk of the boat, a sudden turning of the windlass, and then a second jerk, accompanied by a rapid motion of the boat, made me face round.

'What are you about, Fritz?' I exclaimed, somewhat alarmed.

'I have caught him! — I touched him!' cried Fritz, without hearing. 'The turtle is ours; it cannot escape, father! I have struck him in the neck. Hooray!'

I saw that the harpoon had indeed caught the animal in its only unprotected part, the neck; and, feeling itself wounded, it was trying to get away. I quickly pulled down the sail, and, seizing a hatchet, sprang forward ready to cut the rope, and let the harpoon and the turtle go; but Fritz caught hold of my arm, begging me to wait a moment, and not cut the rope until it was absolutely necessary; and to this I agreed.

So, drawn along by the turtle, we raced dangerously fast through the water. I soon noticed that the creature was making for the sea; I therefore again hoisted the sail, and, as the wind was to the land and very brisk, the turtle found resistance of no avail. He accordingly fell into the track of the current, and drew us straight towards our usual place of landing. The state of the tide was such as to throw us upon a sand-bank; we were at this time close to the shore; the boat, though driven with violence, remained upright in the sand. I stepped into the water, which did not reach far above my knees, and, seeing the turtle stretched at the bottom of the water where it was shallow, I cut off his head with the hatchet. Being now near Tent House, Fritz gave a halloo, and fired a gun to warn the others we had not only arrived, but arrived in triumph. His mother and the three boys soon appeared, running towards us. Our story of the turtle was received with acclamation, only my wife sparing a word of pity for the poor creature so rudely awakened to pain and death.

I sent the younger boys for the sledge, and while they were away made both boat and raft fast, so that the tide should not float them away.

When the sledge arrived we placed the turtle upon it, and also some mattresses, pieces of linen, etc. As we walked up I gave Jack his watch, and Francis his coins, with which he was delighted. As he had lately expressed his intention of sowing some gunpowder to produce a crop, I asked him jestingly if he was going to sow the gold, to which he replied, gravely, no, he should save it up for the next fair, an answer that evoked peals of merriment from his brothers.

Our first thought on reaching home was the turtle, which we immediately turned on his back, that we might strip off the shell, and make use of some of the flesh while it was fresh. Taking my hatchet, I separated the upper and under shell all round. The upper shell is extremely convex; the under, on the contrary, is nearly flat. I cut away as much of the flesh of the animal as was sufficient for a meal, and laid the rest carefully on the under shell, which served as a dish, recommending my wife to cook what I had cut off on the other shell, with no other seasoning than a little salt. She asked to be allowed to cut off the green fat adhering all round, upon which I laughingly told her that that was the greatest delicacy of all, and esteemed at banquets in Europe food for kings. I then rubbed salt on what we meant to keep, and gave the rest to the dogs.

'Oh, dear papa,' cried Francis, 'do give me the shell.'

'No, no,' cried out the others; and one and all claimed it.

I declared that it belonged entirely to Fritz; 'but,' I continued, 'I should like to ask what each of you thought of doing with the shell, if you had got it?'

'I should turn it into a shield to defend myself with, if the savages should come upon us,' said Ernest.

'Pooh!' said Jack. 'There are no savages here! I should make a little boat of it. It would glide along with the stream.'

'I thought,' said Francis in his turn, 'I should build a little house, papa, and the shell would make such a fine roof to it?'

I turned to Fritz:

'And now what use is the rightful owner going to make of it?' I asked.

'I thought,' he replied, 'of cleaning it thoroughly, and fixing it by the side of our river, and keeping it always full of pure water for mother's use, when she has to wash the linen, or cook.'

'Excellent!' I cried, 'the pure water-tub! This is what I call thinking for the general good. And we will do this as soon as we can find some clay, as a solid foundation for its bottom.'

'Ha, ha!' cried Jack, 'I have got some clay. This morning while I was out I came to a large slope by the river, and it was so slippery, that I could not keep upon my legs; so I fell, and dirtied myself all over; on looking, I saw that the ground was of clay, and almost liquid, so I made some of it into balls, and brought them home.'

Ernest was not to be out-done, and declared he too had made a discovery; he had found some roots rather like a horse-radish, which the sow had eaten with relish

From his account, and further particulars I judged them to be *manioc*, or *tapioca*, of which the natives of the West Indies make a sort of bread or cake which they call *cassava*; and I told him if this were so his discovery was of considerable value. We had now finished unloading the sledge, and I bade the three eldest boys accompany me to fetch another load before it should be dark. We left Francis and his mother busy preparing supper.

Having reached the raft, we took from it as much as the sledge could hold, or the animals draw along. One object of my attention was to secure two chests which contained our own clothes, as I well knew this would please my wife. I reckoned also on finding in one of the chests some books on interesting subjects, and principally a large handsomely-printed Bible. I added to these, four cart-wheels and a hand-mill for grinding; which, now that we had discovered the manioc, I considered of importance. These, and a few other articles, completed our present load.

On our return to Falcon's Nest, we found supper ready. Before we began, however, my wife drew me aside by the arm.

'Step this way,' she said, 'and see the work I have done in your absence.'

She pointed to a large cask half sunk in the ground, and covered over with branches of trees. She then applied a small corkscrew to the side, and filling the shell of a coconut with the contents, gave it to me. I found it to be good wine.

'How then,' I asked, 'have you performed this new miracle ?'

She explained to me it was a cask which she had found on the shore, and which the boys had dragged up on the sledge. She had taken this method of keeping the contents cool.

The savoury smell of the turtle now claimed our attention. We hastened back, and all ate heartily of this novel and excellent meat. Afterwards we returned thanks to God, and speedily retired to sleep soundly upon our new mattresses.

CHAPTER XIII

WE GAIN A SAILING BOAT

I ROSE before day to go to the seaside, and look at our boat and raft. I gently descended the ladder without awaking the others. The dogs jumped about me, the cock and the hens flapped their wings and chuckled, and our goats shook their long beards as they browsed. I quickly roused and harnessed the ass, and the dogs followed. As I approached the shore I soon saw that the boat and raft had resisted the tide, though it had partially heaved them up. I got quickly on the raft, took a small loading, and returned to Falcon Stream in time for breakfast. And as no one appeared, though the sun was high above the horizon, I gave a shout as loud as a war-whoop, which awoke my wife.

'Really,' she cried, 'there must be a magic charm in the mattress you brought yesterday, that has lulled us into so sound a sleep!'

Fritz, a little ashamed, was dressed first; Jack soon after him, and Francis next; the ever-slothful Ernest was the last.

Breakfast over, we returned to the seaside to complete the unloading of the raft, that it might be ready for sea on the ebbing of the tide. We were not long in taking two cargoes to Falcon Stream. At our last trip the water was nearly up to our craft. I sent back my wife and the boys, and remained with Fritz till we were quite afloat, when, observing Jack still loitering near, I guessed at his wish, and allowed him to come with us. Shortly after, the tide was high enough for us to row off. Instead of steering for Deliverance Bay to moor our boats there, I was tempted by a fresh sea-breeze to go out again to the wreck; but it was too late to undertake much, and I did not want to pass another night on board. I therefore determined to bring away only what we could pick up easily. Jack was up and down everywhere, and presently he shouted that he had found a wheel-barrow for carrying our potatoes.

But Fritz discovered behind the bulk-head amidship a pinnace — *i.e.*, a small craft, the fore part of which is square — taken to pieces, and two small guns for its defence. This delighted me, but I foresaw that to put it together and launch it would be a Herculean task, so I left it for the time, and collected various utensils, a copper boiler, some plates of iron, tobacco-graters, two grinding-stones, a small barrel of gunpowder, and another full of flints, which I much valued. Jack's barrow was not forgotten; two more were afterwards found and added. All these articles were hurried into the boat, and we re-embarked with speed, to avoid the landwind that rises in the evening. As we were drawing near to the shore we saw a row of small figures ranged on the strand. They were dressed in black, and all uniform, with white waist-coats and full cravats, and looked like a regiment of pigmy soldiers.

Jack suggested they were Lilliputians, such as he had read of in 'Gulliver's Travels.' But as we drew nearer, Fritz cried out that they had beaks, and that their arms were small wings; and in an instant it dawned on us that what we had mistaken for little soldiers were penguins.

While we were talking I steered gently towards shore, and the very moment we got into shallow water Jack leaped in up to his waist, and was quickly on land, hitting right and left with his stick among the penguins, so that half a dozen of them were immediately laid flat; the remainder plunged into the sea, dived, and disappeared.

Arrived at Falcon Stream, my wife showed us a good store of potatoes which she had dug up during our absence, and some of the roots I had taken for manioc or tapioca.

'But now,' I said, 'for supper, and if anyone should be industriously inclined tomorrow I will teach them a new trade.'

I waked the boys very early, reminding them that I had promised to teach them a new trade.

'What is it? What is it?' they all exclaimed at once, springing suddenly out of bed and hurrying into their clothes.

'It is the art of the baker,' I answered. 'Hand me those iron plates that we brought yesterday from the ship, and the tobacco-graters also. Ernest, bring the manioc-root; and I want a small bag made of a piece of strong cloth.'

62

My wife set to work to make one, but she first filled a copper boiler with potatoes and put it on the fire, that we might not be without something to eat at dinner-time if my bread-making turned out a failure. In the meanwhile, I spread a piece of coarse linen on the ground, and, giving each of the boys a grater, showed him how to grate the roots of manioc. In a short time we had produced a considerable heap of shavings like those of horse-radish. They were much amused, saying to each other:

'Will you eat a bit of nice cake made of grated radishes?'

By this time my wife had made the bag. I filled it with the shavings, and she sewed up the end. I now wanted a kind of press. So I cut a long, stout branch from a neighbouring tree, and stripped it of the bark, and placing the bag on our table, put one end of the bough under an arch at about the height of the table, bringing the bough across the bag and pressing down the other end with all my might. After a few seconds of this pressure the sap from the manioc began to run out across the table and drip on to the ground.

After we had wrung out all the sap possible, we opened the bag, and took out a small quantity of the tapioca, and, after stirring the rest about with a stick, replaced it under the press. The next thing was to fix one of our iron plates upon two blocks of stone. Under this we lighted a large fire, and when the iron plate was hot, I made dough by moistening the tapioca flour with water, and put some of it on the plate. As soon as the cake began to be brown underneath, it was turned, that the other side might be baked also.

'Oh, how nice it smells!' cried Ernest eagerly.

As soon as the cake was cold, we broke some of it into crumbs, and gave it to two of the fowls, and a larger piece to the monkey, who nibbled it delightedly, while the boys stood by envying him, for I had decided they must wait a little while to see that there were no ill-effects before tasting it themselves. For dinner, therefore, we had potatoes, and afterwards, finding that the monkey and the fowls were perfectly well, we returned to the bag of manioc.

A large fire was quickly lighted, and when at last the cakes were baked everyone of us enjoyed them very much.

The rest of the day was employed by the boys in making several turns with their wheelbarrows, and by myself in different arrangements in which the ass and our raft had a principal share, both being employed in drawing to Tent House the remaining articles we had brought from the ship.

63

From the time of discovering the pinnace, my desire to have it had been irresistible; but I saw I should have to take the three eldest boys to help me in such a difficult job; and it was some time before I dared tell this to my wife. When I did, however, she agreed on condition we returned the same day. This we promised, and we started cheerfully.

Ernest had not yet been to the ship at all, and was delighted to go. We took with us ample provision of boiled potatoes and the new bread, which I called by the same name savages use for it, namely, *cassava*. We reached the ship easily, but on examining the pinnace were rather dismayed to find the extreme difficulty of the task before us.

The pieces, it is true, were all numbered, but many of them were so heavy I did not see how we were going to move them. We set to work, however, with great energy, in spite of which, when evening came on, we seemed to have done but little. On reaching Deliverance Bay, we found my wife and little Francis there. They had been making, arrangements for our living at Tent House as long as we went backwards and forwards to the ship.

We passed a whole week in this difficult work, going every morning and returning every evening.

At length the pinnace was built up, and ready to be launched. But how could we manage this? She was an elegant little vessel, perfect in every part. She had a small neat deck, and her masts and sails were no less exact and perfect than those of a little brig. We had pitched and caulked all the seams. But in spite of the delight we felt at seeing her thus, the great difficulty still remained. The charming little vessel stood fast enclosed within four walls, nor could I imagine how to get her out. At last I thought, as everything else seemed hopeless, we might blow up part of the ship with gunpowder, and so release her. It was a dangerous thing to try, but it seemed the only way. Accordingly, I made a train and laid a charge of gunpowder under the bulkhead, which blocked in the pinnace on one side. When it was arranged, I set fire to the train, which was long enough to give us time to escape. Then I hurried on board the raft, into which I had previously sent the boys, who had no suspicion of what I had done.

On our arrival at Tent House, I put the raft in order, that we might be able to return to the wreck, when the noise of the explosion should tell me that the scheme had succeeded. Suddenly it came with such violence that my wife and the boys were alarmed.

'What can it be? What is the matter? What can have happened?' they all cried at once.

After a few minutes I explained the real cause, and invited them to come back with me to see what the effect had been. They sprang on board, and we rowed out of the bay more rapidly than ever before. We saw the ship was still afloat, but on rowing round to the far side, where the explosion had taken place, we found that the greater part was shivered to pieces. In the middle of the splinters there floated our pinnace, quite untouched. We all exclaimed joyfully at the complete success of the manoeuvre, and set to work to clear away the wreckage in which she was still entangled.

Two whole days more were spent in completely equipping and loading her. When she was ready for sailing, we decided to salute my wife as we sailed home to Tent House, with two discharges from the cannon, which formed part of the equipment of the pinnace. These accordingly were loaded, and the two young boys stood close to the touch-holes, to be in readiness. Fritz was by the mast to manage the ropes and cables, while I took my station at the rudder. The wind was favourable, and so brisk that we glided swiftly along the water in a very different way from that we were used to on our old tub-boat, which we now towed behind.

When we arrived within a certain distance of the shore, cried Commander Fritz, 'Fire!' Ernest and Jack obeyed, and the echoes from the rocks majestically replied. Fritz at the same moment had discharged his two pistols, and all joined in three loud hurrahs.

'Welcome! welcome!' cried the anxious mother, almost breathless with astonishment and joy. 'Welcome!' cried little Francis, in imitation.

They ran to meet us, and when they had stepped upon the deck the boys begged to fire off the cannon again, and to christen the pinnace by the name of their mother — *The Elizabeth* — a request that I gladly granted.

When the excitement of our arrival had subsided, we found that the two left on shore had done hardly less than ourselves in the last week, for they showed us a kitchen-garden, laid out properly in beds and walks, and sown with the seed of useful plants. One bed was for potatoes, one for manioc, and other smaller ones for lettuces of various kinds, and some plants of the sugar-cane. On the slope of the rock were some plants of the bananas. Between these were some melon seeds; here was a plot allotted to peas and beans, and there another for all sorts of cabbage. Round each bed or plot were sown seeds of maize to serve as a border, to protect the young plants from the heat of the sun. Needless to say, we were delighted by an idea so useful and so well carried out, that it came second only to our securing the pinnace.

Many other matters now required attention, for we had obtained the greater part of the cargo of the ship; but almost all of it was at present in the open air, and liable to injury from both sun and rain. We therefore began to place the cargo safely under shelter along with our other stores.

The pinnace was anchored on the shore, and fastened with a rope, by her head, to a stake. When all our stores were thus disposed of, we began our journey to Falcon Stream, taking with us everything that seemed to be absolutely wanted for comfort, and we found that meant a good deal to carry.

CHAPTER XIV

ADVENTURES AND EXCITEMENT

WHEN we had been once again settled at Falcon's Nest for some days I suggested to the boys that they should practise shooting with arrows; also running, jumping, getting up trees, both by means of climbing up the trunk or by a suspended rope, as sailors are obliged to do to get to the masthead.

We began at first by making knots in the rope, at a foot's distance from each other; then we reduced the number of knots, and before we left off we managed without any. I next taught them a new exercise, which was to throw two balls made of lead, fastened to each end of a string about six feet in length. This was in imitation of the Patagonians, who become so clever by practice that they can throw the balls and string so as to entangle the legs of wild animals and bring them to the ground. The boys were all delighted with the idea and anxious to practise.

My first throws were quite successful, and the string with the balls at the end knotted itself round the little tree at which I had flung it. In a short time Fritz, who was the cleverest at this kind of thing, became quite expert in the art, and took his balls with him wherever he went.

The next morning, as I was dressing, I noticed that the sea was very rough and great waves were rolling in. I stayed at the camp, therefore, all day and made a minute examination of all our various possessions at Falcon Stream. After this I planted the young fruit-trees we had brought from the ship, and the day passed quickly and pleasantly. In the evening I proposed that we should start early next morning, and go to the wood where the gourds grew, as we were in want of more dishes.

By sunrise the next day all were on foot. The donkey was harnessed to the sledge, on which we placed provisions and some powder and shot. Turk led the way as our advanced guard, next followed the three eldest boys; after them, their mother, leading Francis; and Flora brought up the rear, with the monkey on her back.

We set out, full of good humour and high-spirits. Turning round Flamingo Marsh we soon reached the pleasant spot which had before so delighted us. Fritz sent Turk into the tall grass and followed himself. Presently we heard Turk barking loudly; a large bird sprang up, and almost at the same moment a shot from Fritz brought it down, but, though wounded, it was not killed, and set off quickly, not flying, but running. Turk followed, and, seizing it, held it fast till Fritz came up. The bird was large and strong, it kicked so vigorously that Fritz dared not approach it. I saw that it was a female bustard of the largest size. I had long wished to tame a bird of this kind for our poultry-yard; so I threw my pocket handkerchief over its head, and passed a string with a running-knot over its legs; this I drew tight. Then, releasing its wing from Turk's mouth, I tied it, with its fellow, close to the bird's body. Ernest and Jack, who had been behind, now ran forward, shouting:

'Oh, what a handsome bird! and what a size! What beautiful feathers!'

I put the bustard on the sledge, making it as comfortable as I could; and after this little delay we went on our way.

We were compelled to fight our way through thick bushes, till we arrived at the wood of gourds, where we decided to rest a little.

Jack and Ernest collected dried branches and flints, while their mother was occupied in attending to the bustard. She thought that it was cruel to keep it any longer blinded, with its legs tied together. So, to please her, I loosened the string, but still left it partly tied. Then I fastened the bird by a long string to the trunk of a tree.

We now began our work. Some had to cut, others to saw, scoop out, and model the gourds into shape.

After working for some time with the rest, Ernest, who was not fond of continuous work, wandered into the wood. It was not long before we heard him calling loudly to us, and saw him running back.

'Run quick, father!' he cried; 'here is a wild boar — a terrible beast!'

67

I cried out to the boys to call the dogs quickly. But when we turned in chase the boar was gone, and we saw nothing but a plot of potatoes in which he had been rooting. The dogs tracked him, and their yells soon told us he had been discovered. As Fritz and I emerged with caution from the undergrowth, holding our guns at full-cock, we burst simultaneously into fits of laughter; for the terrific beast was not a boar at all, but our own sow, which had run away and been so long lost!

While we were still chaffing Ernest about the incident, we noticed a kind of small apple, which seemed to have fallen from the trees and lay thickly in the grass. Our attention was attracted to them by the way in which the sow ate them; and we collected some to take home to try upon the monkey.

We now began to be extremely thirsty, and scattered in search of water. Jack sprang off, and sought among the rocks, hoping to find a stream; but scarcely had he left the wood than he shouted to us that he had found a crocodile.

'A crocodile!' I cried, with a hearty laugh; 'you have a fine imagination, my boy! Whoever saw a crocodile on such scorching rocks as these, with not a drop of water near? Now, Jack, you are surely dreaming —'

'Not so much of a dream as you may think, father,' answered Jack, trying to speak in a low voice, 'Fortunately he is asleep; he lies here on a stone at his full length. Come here and look at him; he does not stir in the least.'

We stole softly to the place where the animal lay; but, instead of a crocodile, I saw before me a sort of lizard, named by naturalists *Leguana*, or *Iguana*, of an enormous size, about eight feet in length, including the tail. Fritz was already taking aim with his gun, but I prevented him, wishing to try an experiment.

I cut a stout stick from a bush, and, tying a string with a running knot to the end of it, approached the creature with cautious steps. When I was very near to him I began to whistle a lively tune, taking care to make the sounds low at first, and to increase in loudness till the lizard was awaked. He appeared entranced with pleasure, raising his head eagerly and looking round on all sides. I now advanced by a step at the time. At length I was near enough to reach him with a switch, with which I tickled him gently, still continuing to whistle. The lizard stretched himself at full length, made motions with his long tail, threw his head about, raised it up, and disclosed a range of sharp pointed teeth. I seized the moment of his raising his head to throw my noose over him. When this was accomplished, it was the work of a moment

68

to draw it tight and strangle him at once. As his flesh is good for eating, we had next to consider the best way of transporting him to Falcon Stream. The only way, it seemed, was to carry him on my back, but he was so large that when his fore paws were on my shoulders his tail dragged on the ground. Thus equipped, looking as if I wore a royal mantle of green and gold, I returned to where we had made a temporary camp.

While we were sitting by the others, recounting this strange adventure, some of the little apples fell from my pockets, and lay on the ground by my side. Nip soon scented them; he came slyly up, and, stealing several, began eating them with great eagerness. I myself threw one or two to the bustard, which also ate them without hesitation. So I told the boys they might as well follow this example, and we all ate them with much enjoyment. I began to suspect that they were the sort of fruit called *guava*.

We had scarcely finished before my wife asked that we might begin our journey home, and as the evening was so far advanced, she suggested that we should leave the sledge, which was heavily laden, to be fetched the following day. I agreed, and loaded the donkey with the bags which contained our new gourds; the lizard, which I feared might not keep fresh; and little Francis, began to complain of being tired. As for the bustard, she walked, led by a string.

Our course lay through a wood of majestic oaks, and the ground was covered with acorns, upon which numerous birds seemed to subsist. This we gathered from the wild and discordant cries of several sorts of jays and parrots, which were hopping merrily among the foliage and the branches.

We arrived shortly at Falcon Stream, and finished the exertions of the day with a good supper, and after making a comfortable bed for the bustard by the side of the flamingo, we stretched our weary limbs upon our beds in the giant tree.

CHAPTER XV

THE LAST OF THE WRECK

I HAD left the sledge behind for two reasons, not only to save the tired donkey, but to give me an excuse for going back into the woods with Fritz, to explore a little further. So, taking Turk with us, he and I started directly after breakfast the next morning.

We soon arrived at the place where we had left the sledge, which we found untouched. Then we made our way to the line of cliff-like rocks beyond which we had not yet penetrated.

On the way we went through a grove, the trees of which were unknown to us. Their branches were loaded with berries covered with sticky wax. I knew of a sort of bush producing wax that grows in America, and had no doubt that this was the plant, which might prove very useful. We set to work, therefore, and gathered as many of the berries as we could carry, for I told Fritz I believed I could make candles from them.

Soon after we came upon some trees like the wild fig-tree. Their height was from forty to sixty feet, and a kind of gum oozed from the trunks. Fritz collected some of this, and as we walked he pulled it about like elastic or gutta-percha. Seeing this it dawned upon me what the gum really was, namely, India rubber which might by a little trouble be made very useful to us.

Our next discovery was of a tree called the sago palm. One of these had been blown down by the wind, so that I was able to examine it thoroughly. I found that the trunk contained some mealy stuff, therefore with my hatchet I cut it open longways and cleared it of the contents; and I found on tasting it was exactly like the sago I had often eaten. Thus we had made in a short time three very remarkable and useful discoveries.

We now began to consider how much further we would go; the thick bushes of bamboo, through which it was impossible to pass, seemed to put an end to our exploration, so we turned to the left towards Cape Disappointment, where were the plantations of sugar-canes. We cut a large bundle of the canes, which we threw across the donkey's back, and then soon arrived on the seashore; after this we returned to the sledge, and harnessing the donkey, turned homewards.

The next day the first thing that came into my mind when I awoke was the promise to try my hand at candle-making. After breakfast I asked my wife to make some wicks of sail-cloth, and meantime I put some berries into a pan over the fire. When I saw an oily matter rise to the top of the pan, I carefully skimmed it off and put it aside, still keeping it liquid and melted near the fire. I continued this process till I had collected a considerable amount of wax. Then I dipped the wicks one by one into it, and hung them on the bushes to harden. In a short time I dipped them again, and repeated the operation till the candles were the proper size, when I put them aside to cool. We were all eager to try them, and when we did so, we found they gave quite a good light.

This success made me think of something else, namely, to make butter of our cream. But we had no churn. I remembered, however, something I had read, and emptying a large gourd, I filled it with cream, and placing it on a piece of sail-cloth with four corners, I tied each corner to a stake, and told the boys to stand beside it and shake it. They sang and laughed all the time, and in an hour we found the cream really had turned to butter.

The next thing I had in my mind was to make a cart, as we had some wheels. I cannot say that this was a very brilliant performance, but still, after considerable time and labour, we did succeed in making something which was better than the sledge.

In the next few days we went over to Tent House, and planted a hedge of prickly-pear round it, and made it into a kind of fortress in case we were ever attacked by savages.

At last it seemed to me it was about time to go back to the ship, which still held together on the rocks, so I took the three eldest boys with me and made another trip. We secured some chests of clothes, and whatever remained of powder, shot, and even such pieces of cannon as we could remove.

It was necessary to spend several days in visits to the ship, returning in the evening, bringing everything likely to be useful; in this we included doors, windows, locks, bolts, so that the ship was now entirely emptied. Then I made up my mind to blow up the wreck, so that the boards themselves might drift on shore. This we performed successfully, and though we felt a little sad at seeing the last of the dear old ship, we were satisfied we had done rightly.

The morning after we found the shore strewn with wreckage, and the drawing up and stowing away of the planks, etc., was very hard work. When we had put everything in order we returned to Falcon's Nest.

CHAPTER XVI

THE TROOP OF BUFFALOES

AFTER a little rest the desire for exploration came once more strongly upon us. This time it was decided all should go, and that we should take enough requisites for staying away the night, in case we required them.

We took the cart, though we had some difficulty in getting it through the bushes down to the seashore, and followed the same track by which Fritz and I had returned the last time. When we reached the India rubber trees, I cut incisions in the trunks at various heights, and placed beneath them gourds, so that the milky juice dripping down, might harden into gum.

When we arrived at the bay formed by Cape Disappointment we decided to make a temporary camp here. So we unharnessed the animals, and left them to graze, and as it was now evening, began to think about our own supper.

Suddenly the stillness was broken by the loud braying of the donkey, and we saw him throwing his head in the air, and kicking and prancing about; then he set off at a full gallop. We began to fear that some wild beast might be near, and I hurried out with Fritz and the two dogs in the direction the donkey had taken.

In spite of an anxious search, we could find nothing, and returned to the camp vexed by the loss of our valuable donkey. The boys had made a pleasant hut with sail-cloth in the meantime, and seated before it on the sand in the warm glow of the fire we enjoyed our supper, and forgot our annoyance.

The night passed safely, though I took care to get up from time to time to make up the fires, so as to scare away any wild animals, and in the morning, after breakfasting on milk, boiled potatoes, and Dutch cheese, we decided that one of the boys and myself should seek the donkey. I chose Jack, who was delighted to come on such an errand.

We soon reached the bamboo plantation, and after some time we discovered the marks of the donkey's hoofs. After spending a whole hour in tracing them we arrived at the edge of the plantation, saw the sea in the distance, and soon after found ourselves in an open space, which bounded the great bay. A river flowed into the sea at this place, and we saw that the ridge of rocks ended in a perpendicular precipice, leaving only a narrow passage at the end, which during every tide must be under water, but which at that moment was dry. We went round this corner, and when we got to the other side we found the mark of the donkey's hoofs again on the sand. But we saw with astonishment that they were not alone, but mingled with many others larger, but very like them.

By climbing a hill we were able to see a long way, and in the far distance discerned what seemed to be a herd of animals. Drawing nearer we discovered them to be buffaloes. By good luck the dogs were far behind us, and though the buffaloes saw us, they gave no sign of fear or of displeasure at our approach; they stood perfectly still, with their large round eyes fixed upon us in vacant surprise; those which were lying down got up slowly, but they did not seem fierce.

Unfortunately at that minute Turk and Flora ran up to us, and the buffaloes instantly, and all together, set up such a roar as to make us tremble; they struck their horns and their hoofs upon the ground, which they tore up in pieces and scattered in the air. Turk and Flora, fearless of danger, ran right into the middle of them, and seizing the ears of a young buffalo, dragged him towards us. With palpitating hearts and trembling hands we fired both at the same moment; the buffaloes, terrified by the sound and by the smoke, remained for an instant motionless, as if struck by a thunderbolt, and then rushed away, and were soon beyond the reach of sight. Only one stayed behind, a female, who was no doubt the mother of the young buffalo which the dogs still kept a prisoner. She had been wounded, and now rushed furiously at the dogs. I aimed carefully and, luckily, killed her at the first shot.

I was wondering what we could do with the young buffalo, who bellowed and foamed with rage, when Jack suddenly pulled out of his pocket his string with balls at the ends, and throwing it skilfully, entangled the buffalo's legs and brought him to the ground.

But, by this action, the difficulty was only partly solved. The question was now how we were to get him home. I remembered a way practised with bulls in Spain, which, though cruel, is effective, and I decided to use it. I took from my pocket a sharp-pointed knife, and, seizing his nose, I made a hole in the nostril, into which I quickly inserted a string; this I immediately tied to a tree, so that the animal was prevented from moving his head.

Then I called off the dogs, and, trying a few minutes after, found that he was ready to follow the pull of the cord, which hurt his nose. Having settled this I left him tied up and turned to the dead buffalo. I first cut out the tongue, next took off the skin, and lastly, cut off some of the flesh, and salted it, and left the rest to the dogs. I then went to the river to wash myself, after which we sat down under the shade of a large tree, and ate the provisions we had brought with us.

When we were ready to go home, I untied the young buffalo, and found that he followed me without resistance. He was so quiet that when we tied a bundle of large reeds, that we had cut, to his back, he did not seem to mind. We re-passed the river in safety, and regained the narrow pass at the turn of the rocks. On arriving at the camp, question after question was showered upon us. All agreed that our success with the buffalo was most extraordinary; and they were never tired of examining him.

While we had been away, Fritz had caught a young eagle that he thought he might train to hunt like a falcon. I was doubtful of his being able to accomplish this, and when he had finished talking I made a fire and put a good deal of green wood on it to make a thick smoke, over which I meant to hang the buffalo meat I had salted, to preserve for our future use. The young buffalo was beginning to browse, and we gave him some milk and mashed potatoes, which he ate willingly. Early next morning we were ready to return to Falcon Stream. Our buffalo was yoked with the cow, and was very tractable. It is true I led him by the cord in his nose, and this kept him in check. We returned the same way as we came, and reached the wax and gum trees without any accident. The elastic gum had not yielded as much as I expected, but we got enough to make a pair of waterproof boots as I had wished. On the way back we had another alarm on account of our old sow, who now appeared with a litter of seven little ones, a sight I was pleased to see.

On arriving at Falcon Stream, Fritz incautiously uncovered the eyes of his eaglet, which became unmanageable, and would have been lost altogether had not Ernest suggested stupefying it by the fumes of tobacco-smoke, a method of which he had read. This experiment proved so successful that the monkey was given to him by Fritz as a reward.

For a long time I had felt that the rope ladder, which led to our home in the tree, was a difficult and dangerous mode of ascent, and the idea of cutting steps in the tree itself now occurred to me. The boys had talked of a hollow in the trunk, from which a swarm of bees issued, and so I determined to see whether the hole extended to the roots. The boys climbed up like squirrels to strike at the trunk with axes; but they soon paid dearly for their attempt, the whole swarm of bees flew out, buzzing with fury, and attacked them savagely. Jack struck fiercely at them, and was more severely attacked by them than the rest; so badly was he stung, that it was necessary to cover the whole of his face with linen, and some hours elapsed before even the other boys could open their eyes. The bees, in the meantime, were still buzzing furiously round the tree. I determined to smoke them out, so, waiting until they quieted down, and had returned to their home, I stopped the passages with clay, leaving only one hole. I then smoked into this with one of the clay pipes we had brought from the ship. At first a humming was heard in the hollow of the tree, and a noise like a gathering tempest, but it died away by degrees. When all was calm I withdrew my pipe. We then began, with a chisel and a small axe, to cut out of the tree, under the bees' hole of entrance, a piece three feet square. This I took out from the trunk like a window, and we saw such a stock of wax and honey, that we were astonished. The whole of the tree was lined with fine honeycombs. I cut them off with care, and put them in the gourds which the boys handed to me.

When I had somewhat cleared the cavity, I put the upper combs, in which the bees had assembled in clusters and swarms, into the gourd which was to serve as a hive. All this time the bees remained quite motionless and stupefied. Then I came down, bringing with me the rest of the honeycombs, with which I filled a small cask, which had been previously well washed in the stream.

Having placed the gourds like hives on a plank, I fumigated the inside of the tree thoroughly with tobacco, to prevent the bees returning. This answered perfectly. At first, when they recovered from their stupor, they flew back to the tree, but soon returned to their new hives, where the queen was, and settled there.

Having now discovered that the tree was almost entirely hollow, I intended to make my staircase inside it. I first fixed in the centre the trunk of a tree completely stripped of its branches, in order to carry my winding staircase round it. On the outside of this trunk and the inside of our own tree, we cut niches to hold the boards which would make steps. I made another hole to serve as a window, and larger ones to form doors at the top and bottom. I fixed the windows taken from the captain's cabin in the smaller holes. But all this took a long time, and many things happened during its progress.

To the boys' delight Flora presented us with two puppies. A few days later the two she-goats gave us two kids, and our sheep five lambs, so that now we had quite a flock.

Next to the winding stairs, my chief occupation was the young buffalo, whose nose was now quite healed, so that I could lead it at will with a cord or stick. I preferred the stick, which answered the purpose of a bit, and I resolved to break in this spirited beast for riding as well as drawing. It was already used to the shafts, and behaved very well in them; but I had more trouble in teaching it to be a saddle-horse. I formed a sort of saddle with sail-cloth, and upon this I fixed a burden, which I increased daily. The monkey was the first rider, and he stuck so close to the saddle, that in spite of the plunging and kicking of the buffalo, he was not thrown. Francis was then tried, as the lightest of the family, and managed very well. Jack now showed impatience to mount, so I passed the stick through the buffalo's nose, and tied strong packthread to each end of it, and put this bridle into his hands. For a time he kept on the saddle, notwithstanding the wild antics of his steed; but at last he was thrown, without being hurt. He was quite ready to try again, and then Fritz had his turn; so at last the buffalo got used to carrying one or the other of us, and so strong was it, that the three eldest boys could mount together, and it hardly seemed to feel their weight.

Fritz, meantime, did not neglect his eagle. He taught it to perch on his wrist whenever he called or whistled to it; but some time elapsed before he could trust it to soar without holding it by a long string to bring it back.

When I had completed the staircase, I turned my attention to the making of a pair of rubber boots.

CHAPTER XVII

THE TRAINING OF A WILD ASS

WE were scarcely up one morning when we heard strange noises that resembled the howlings of wild beasts. Our dogs pricked up their ears, and we loaded our guns and pistols, and looked at each other anxiously.

The howlings were presently renewed much closer to us. Fritz listened attentively, and then burst out laughing, exclaiming:

'Father, it is our donkey. Listen! do you not hear his brayings?'

I listened, and a fresh roar, in sounds unquestionable, raised loud peals of laughter amongst us. Shortly after we saw our old friend Grizzle moving towards us, stopping now and then to browse; but to our surprise he was accompanied by one of his own species, much more graceful than himself. I knew it to be a fine onagra, or wild ass.

So I got ready at once a long cord with a running knot, one end of which I tied fast to the root of a tree. This I entrusted to Fritz, as he was more skilful in throwing it than I was. The two animals drew nearer and nearer to us. Fritz, holding in his hand the open noose, moved softly on from behind the tree where we were concealed. The onagra started at first on seeing him. It sprang backwards, then stopped to examine the unknown form; but as Fritz now remained quite still, the animal resumed its composure, and continued to browse. Soon after he approached the donkey, and held out a handful of oats.

Grizzle ran up to take his favourite food, and the stranger drew near, raised its head, and eventually came so close that Fritz, seizing the opportunity, succeeded in throwing the rope round its neck, but the motion so frightened the animal that it instantly sprang off. It was soon checked by the cord, which drew tight, and almost strangled it. It could go no farther, and, after many exhausting efforts, it sank panting upon the ground. I loosened the cord, and quickly threw our donkey's halter over its head; then I fixed in its nose a split cane that I had previously got ready. This had the effect of a pair of pincers. I fastened the halter with two long ropes to two roots near us, and let the animal recover itself.

In a few moments the onagra got up and kicked wildly; but the pain of its nose, which was grasped and violently squeezed in the bamboo, forced it to lie down again. Meantime we caught and tied up Grizzle, fastening him near the wild ass, and put before both plenty of good food.

For days, however, the onagra remained savage and shy. I let the nippers remain on its nose, for without them no one could have approached it. I took them off, however, at times when I gave it food, and I began, as with the buffalo, by placing a bundle of sail-cloth on its back. The children came by turns to play with it and scratch its ears gently. But for a long time we despaired of success; the onagra made furious starts and leaps when any of us went near it, kicked with its hind feet, and even attempted to bite those who touched it. This obliged me to have recourse to a muzzle, which I managed to fix on. To avoid being kicked I tied the fore feet and hind feet together. At length it grew tamer, and was no longer in a rage when we approached, but bore being handled and stroked.

At last we ventured to free it by degrees from its restraints, and to ride it as we had done with the buffalo, still keeping the fore feet tied; but, notwithstanding this precaution, it proved as fierce and unruly as ever. The monkey, who was first put on its back, held on pretty well by clinging to its mane, while the onagra furiously reared and plunged, but it was impossible for any of the boys to mount. When tied up the onagra seemed tolerably quiet and gentle, but the moment it was in any degree unshackled it became wholly ferocious and unmanageable.

I was at length reduced to my last chance, and I made up my mind that, if it did not answer, I would set the animal at liberty. I tried to mount the onagra, and, as it reared to prevent me, I seized one of its long ears with my teeth, and bit it till it bled. The onagra became motionless and as stiff as a stake. Fritz seized the moment, and sprang on its back; Jack, with the help of his mother, did the same, holding on by his brother. Then I let go of the ear; the onagra made a few springs, but, checked by the cords on its feet, it gradually submitted, began to trot up and down more quietly, and at last grew tractable.

I explained to the boys that I had heard of this extraordinary mode of taming from a horse-breaker I met with by chance, who had found it sometimes the only method when all others had failed.

During the training of our steed, which we named Lightfoot, our hens had given us a crowd of chickens; forty of these, at least, were chirping and hopping about us, to the great satisfaction of my wife.

This reminded us of a project we had long thought of, namely — to build covered sheds for all our animals. The rainy season, which is the winter of these countries, was drawing near, so we could not delay.

We had plenty of planks at our disposal, and our experience of carpentering enabled us to complete the work without any very great difficulty, though it took some time.

In one of his rambles Ernest had picked some long, flat leaves which he called sword-grass. When I examined these I began to suspect that here was a real treasure; nothing less than flax, from which we could make the thread of which my wife had felt the need, and from which she could eventually spin linen. The boys willingly returned to the place where Ernest had made his find, and brought back bundles of the precious plant.

But there was much to be done before we could make use of the leaves. The first process was that they had to be soaked. For this purpose we carried them to Flamingo Marsh and left them there in the water for a fortnight.

After this we took them out and spread them on the grass in the sun. Occasional slight showers, showing that the wet season was near, had already come on. The temperature, which hitherto had been warm and serene, became gloomy and variable; the sky was often darkened with clouds, the stormy winds were heard.

It was necessary to lay in a stock of everything we should want for the next few months. So we dug up a supply of potatoes and yams for bread, with plenty of coconuts, and some bags of sweet acorns.

Our cart was incessantly in motion, conveying home our winter stock. Time was so precious that we did not even make regular meals, and limited ourselves to bread, cheese, and fruits, in order to shorten them, and to return quickly to our work, and despatch it before the bad season should set in. Unfortunately, the weather changed sooner than we had expected. Before we had completed our winter establishment the rain fell in heavy torrents.

The first thing to be done was to fix our residence at the bottom of the tree, between the roots and under the tarred roof I had erected; for it was no longer possible to remain above on account of the furious winds. We took down our hammocks, mattresses, and every article that could be injured by the rain; and most fortunate did we deem ourselves in having made the winding stairs, which served as a kind of lumber room. Our little sheds between the roots, constructed for the poultry and the cattle, could scarcely contain us all; and the first days we passed in them we were very uncomfortable, crowded all together, and hardly able to move. We were half stifled with smoke whenever we lit a fire, and drenched with rain when we opened the doors. The staircase was, as I have said, very useful. The upper part of it was filled with numerous articles; and as it was lighted and sheltered by windows, my wife often worked there seated on a stair, with little Francis at her feet.

As to the smoke, our only remedy was to open the door to get rid of it; and we lived on milk and cheese as much as possible, never making a fire but to bake our cakes, when we used the opportunity to boil enough potatoes and salt meat to last us several days. A more serious difficulty was our not having provided sufficient hay and leaves for the cow, the ass, the sheep, and goats, so that we had to give them our potatoes and sweet acorns. Fortunately we had laid in a sufficient stock of candles, and when darkness obliged us to light up, we sat round the table, where a large taper fixed on a gourd gave us a good light, so that my wife could sew while I wrote up my journal, and the boys amused themselves with the books we had taken from the Captain's chest; these proved a great resource, and taught them many things about the plants and birds they had lately seen.

Our diet was occasionally varied by a chicken, pigeon, or duck, from our poultry-yard, or some of the thrushes we had preserved in butter, and every four or five days we made fresh butter, and this, with honey spread on our manioc cakes, was a pleasant treat.

Our last job for the winter, undertaken at my wife's solicitation, was a machine called a beetle, for the flax, and some carding combs. These I made with some difficulty, but when finished the drying, peeling, and spinning of the flax became a source of pleasure to my wife.

CHAPTER XVIII

THE SHINING GROTTO

I CAN hardly describe our joy when, after many tedious and gloomy weeks of rain, the sky began to brighten and the wind to drop.

The vegetation of our trees was rapidly advancing; the seed we had thrown into the ground was sprouting in slender blades; the earth was covered with flowers. The song of birds was heard, and they were seen joyfully fluttering from branch to branch.

Our summer occupations began by arranging and thoroughly cleaning Falcon's Nest, which the rain and dead leaves blown by the wind had disturbed; the stairs were cleared, and the rooms between the roots reoccupied. My wife lost not a moment in busying herself with her flax, from which she meant if possible to spin a piece of linen. I carried the bundles of flax into the open air, and made an oven to dry them well. The same evening we all set to work to peel and afterwards to beat the flax and strip off the bark; and lastly, to comb it with my carding machine. I took this task on myself, and drew out distaffs full of long soft flax ready for spinning; my wife was delighted, and wanted me to make her a wheel without delay. It was no easy task, but at last I succeeded, whereupon she fell so eagerly to spinning that she had no time for anything else.

On our first visit to Tent House we found the ravages of winter considerable; the tempest and rain had beaten down the tent, and made havoc amongst our provisions. Luckily our handsome pinnace was safe, but our tub-boat was in too shattered a state to be of any further use.

In looking over the stores we found the gunpowder, of which I had left three barrels in the tent, the most damaged. This gave me the idea of searching for a cavern, in which we might store the remainder more safely. After hunting carefully in all directions we found a hole which, though not large in itself, seemed to form the entrance to a mighty grotto. I despatched Jack on the buffalo to Falcon Stream, to tell his mother and brothers of our discovery, directing him to return with them, and bring all the tapers that were left, so that we might explore it.

When they arrived I immediately lighted some of the tapers, and gave one to each, and thus we entered the rock in solemn procession. We had scarcely advanced four paces within the cave when we all exclaimed with admiration and surprise. The most beautiful and magnificent spectacle presented itself. The sides of the cavern sparkled like diamonds, the light from our six tapers was reflected from all parts, and had the effect of a grand illumination. Innumerable crystals hung from the top of the vault, which, joining with others at the sides, formed pillars, altars, and all sorts of fantastic shapes. In some places all colours of the rainbow shone from the angles of the crystals, and gave them the appearance of the finest precious stones.

Our astonishment was so great as to be almost ludicrous; we seemed in a kind of dumb stupor, half imagining it was a dream. For my own part, I had seen stalactites, and read the description of famous grottoes, but I had never pictured anything so marvellous. Jack cried out he was in a cathedral; Francis declared it to be a fairy palace, and his mother named it the House of Diamonds. The ground was level, covered with a white and very fine sand. I broke off a bit of the nearest crystal, and, tasting it, found it to be of pure salt.

As we advanced into the grotto, remarkable figures showed on every side; columns reached from the bottom to the top of the vault; here and there undulating masses like lace shawls; others appeared like large open cupboards, benches, church ornaments, grotesque figures of men and animals; some like polished crystals or diamonds, others like blocks of alabaster.

We viewed with delighted curiosity this strange sight, and loud exclamations succeeded astonishment. Many schemes were formed for converting this magnificent grotto into a new home; for though there was no need for our immediate removal there, it would be an invaluable storehouse, and make a snug retreat for the next rainy season.

Partly by the use of gunpowder and partly by hewing, we succeeded in a few weeks' time in making doors and windows in the front wall. In these we fixed the window-frames and doorways we had brought from the ship, and inside we divided the cavern by wooden partitions into several rooms. I kept the finest of the pillars, and the most beautiful pieces to decorate what would be our winter drawing-room. The large ones served us for chairs and tables; their shining crystals multiplied the reflection of the lights. We divided the cave into two parts by a partition; the one on the right was to be our residence; that on the left was to contain the kitchen, stables, and work-room. At the end of the second division, where windows could not be placed, the cellar and store-room were to be formed; the whole separated by partition-boards, with doors of communication. The living-room was again subdivided into three: the first, next the door, was the bedroom for my wife and me; the second a dining-room, and the last a bedroom for the boys. As we had only three windows, we put one in each sleeping-room; the third was fixed in the kitchen, where my wife would often be. I made a good fireplace in the kitchen, near the window; also I pierced the rock a little above, and the hole answered the purpose of a chimney. Lastly came the stables, which were divided into four compartments, and occupied all the bottom of the cavern on one side; on the other were the cellar and magazine.

During the long stay we made at Tent House we had several advantages. Immense turtles were often seen on the shore, where they deposited their eggs in the sand, and these we appropriated. Sea-lobsters, oysters, and many other smaller fishes we could catch in any number.

One morning at some distance from the shore the water seemed in a state of commotion; many birds hovered over it, sometimes they darted along the surface of the water, sometimes rose in the air, flying in a circle, pursuing each other in every direction. At first we were much puzzled by this, but at last I guessed what it meant, and exclaimed that it was a shoal of herrings about to enter Deliverance Bay.

By this time the shoal of herrings were nearing us. They made a loud rustling noise in the water, leaping over each other, and displaying their silver scales. We all rushed into the water; the boys used the largest gourds as pails, dipping them in and bringing them out full of fish. These they emptied into the shattered old tubs that had once formed our boat. When we were all exhausted with the hard work the shoal passed onward.

Then we had the disagreeable task of cleaning and salting our catch before us. Luckily, we had now plenty of salt, and, as we all joined in the work, it was not long before we had several barrels full of properly cured fish.

Scarcely had we finished our salting, when another excitement claimed us. A number of fish called sea-dogs, that had followed the herrings came into the bay and river. These fish were not good for eating, but their skins, tanned and dressed, make excellent leather. I was in great need of it for straps and harness. Besides, I knew the fat yielded good lamp oil, so we took pains to catch them.

We were again successful, and in a short time we had secured a sufficient number of them, and carefully preserved the fat.

Pleased with the operations of the week, we set out all together cheerfully for Falcon Stream, to pass our Sunday there.

We found everything here in an equally good condition. Our grain had sprung up with an almost incredible rapidity and luxuriance, and was now nearly ready for reaping. Barley, wheat, rye, oats, peas, millet, lentils, were all growing — only a small quantity of each, it is true, but sufficient to enable us to sow again plentifully at the proper season. The plant that had yielded most was maize — a proof that it best loved the soil.

Our feathered colony had increased so much since our arrival on the island that we thought it would not be a bad thing to take one or two of them on our next excursion, and leave them in another part, so that in time they would be able to replenish the whole island. We purposed in this way to make a new farm colony at some distance from Falcon Stream. This we could visit from time to time, and the animals we left there would learn to feed themselves.

We were not long in putting the project into execution. I selected from among the pigs, sheep, fowls, etc., those I deemed healthy, and we placed them in the cart. We followed the usual route, with little deviation, and the only incident that occurred was the discovery of a grove of cotton plants — a most useful acquisition. Little Francis was the first to call our attention to it.

'Look, father,' cried he, 'here is a place full of snow! Let me get down and make some snowballs!'

And, turning, I saw a number of low bushes, covered with what appeared to be patches of snow.

Fritz darted forward on his onagra, and returned with one hand filled with tufts of a most excellent species of cotton. The pods had burst from ripeness, and the winds had scattered around their flaky contents; the ground was strewed with them, they had gathered in tufts on the bushes, and they floated gently in the air.

After this, we soon reached the high ground which we had been making for; behind, a thick forest gradually rose above us, which sheltered us from the north wind; it ended in a plain, clothed luxuriantly with grass, shrubs, and plants, and watered by a stream.

When we had refreshed ourselves with a meal, we pitched our camp there for the night, and, making up the bundles of cotton we had gathered into pillows, went to bed earlier than usual.

CHAPTER XIX

NIP FINDS STRAWBERRIES

I HAD imagined it would take only a couple of days to knock up a rough shed as a shelter for our stock, but when we began we found we liked the place so much that we added also a hut for ourselves; and this work took a whole week, so that our food ran short before we had done. Accordingly I sent Fritz and Jack to Falcon Stream, and to Tent House, to fetch new supplies of cheese, ham, potatoes, dried fish, cassava bread, and also to distribute fresh food to the numerous animals we had left there.

They set off, one on the onagra and the other on the buffalo — a comical couple, delighted with themselves and their errand. While they were absent, Ernest managed to shoot one or two birds, which sufficed for our wants.

Nip also contributed to our board, for he found a bed of strawberries, of an extraordinary size and delightful flavour. As they were fully ripe, these made a great addition to our scanty larder.

The boys returned the next day, having performed their errand well, and brought back abundant supplies.

For some time I had had it in my mind to make a light bark canoe, such as natives use, but I had as yet seen no tree that would answer the purpose, for I wanted a piece of bark no less than eighteen feet by five. However, in the next few days I came across a tree of sufficient size with just the sort of bark I wanted. Accordingly, we made an incision quite round the trunk in two places, and then cut a perpendicular strip. Next we had to insert our tools gently to separate the bark from the trunk without breaking it. At length with joy we saw it lying safely on the grass.

84

Our business was now to mould it to our purpose. I saw we could not do much more with it here, so resolved to take it back to Tent House for further work. We put it on the cart with some difficulty, and though it caused us great anxiety on the journey, we conveyed it home safely.

Two days later, with benches, a small mast and triangular sail, a rudder, and a thick coat of pitch on the outside, we had a real watertight boat.

We had still two months in prospect before the rainy season, and we employed them in completing our abode in the grotto, with the exception of such ornaments as we might have time to think of during the long days of winter.

We plastered over the walls of the principal apartments on each side with the greatest care, finishing them by pressure with a flat, smooth board, and lastly a wash in the manner of the plasters in Europe.

All we had suffered during this season in the preceding year doubled the value of the comforts and conveniences with which we were now surrounded. We were never tired of admiring our warm and well-arranged apartments, lighted with windows, and well secured with doors from wind and rain, and our granary filled with more than a sufficient winter supply of food for ourselves and for our cattle. Instead of dreading the winter, we began to look forward to it.

CHAPTER XX

THE RAINY SEASON

ONE morning, having arisen earlier than the others, I occupied myself by counting up the time that had passed away since our shipwreck. I calculated the dates, and found that the next day would be the anniversary of that event. It was just two years since we had landed on the island. I resolved, therefore, to keep the day as a holiday, and to test the boys in the various physical exercises they had learnt since landing.

They were delighted with the idea, and competed for the prizes I held out with energy and skill. Fritz was the best shot, though with bow and arrows, all, even Francis, did well. Ernest won the long race, as he took it more coolly than his brothers, and did not exhaust himself at the start; and in horsemanship none could equal Jack, though Francis, who suddenly appeared on the young bull, which he had tamed secretly and named 'Storm', ran him close.

In the evening we made a kind of throne for their mother in the grotto, and she awarded the prizes with her usual graciousness. They each received something suitable, beginning with a new rifle for Fritz and ending with a paint-box for Francis.

Before the rainy season set in our cow gave birth to a little calf, and the onagra delighted us by presenting us with a dainty little foal. It was obvious that we must take especial care of these young things during the wet weather that was fast approaching.

The rains had already commenced; several times we had been visited by heavy showers. By degrees the horizon became covered with thick clouds, the winds swept fearfully along the coast, the waves rose, and for the space of fifteen days we were witnesses of a scene of majesty and terrific grandeur. Nature seemed overturned, the trees bent to the terrible blasts, the lightning and the thunder were mingled with the wind and the rain. It seemed to us that the storm of last year had been nothing in comparison with it.

Nevertheless, the winds fell, the rain poured steadily, and we knew it would continue for twelve weeks.

In spite of the great improvement in our quarters upon those of last year, there were many discomforts. There were but three openings in the grotto, besides the door: one in the kitchen, one in the work-room, and a third in my sleeping chamber. The boys' room, and all the rest of our home, was in complete darkness.

To remedy this we planted a large bamboo upright in the centre of the cave, and hung the ship's lantern to the top of it, and as it was reflected by the many stalactites, it gave enough light for general purposes.

We took the opportunity for arranging our little library on shelves; and we made in the work-room a turning-lathe and an anvil and forge, so that we could turn out quite business-like articles. We devoted some hours each day to the study of foreign languages, an arrangement that did not suit the restless Jack at all.

CHAPTER XXI

THE MONSTER WHALE

WITH these occupations we passed the time pleasantly enough, and in spite of the rain we always made a point of taking a run along the beach, or a scramble about the cliffs, every day.

While we were out in this way we saw one day, far along the beach, a dark mass, which we imagined at first to be the hull of an upturned boat, but on investigation it proved to be the body of a dead whale drifted up by the waves. We put some empty barrels in our boat, and, launching it, sailed along, and landed near the monster, which was between sixty and seventy feet long.

I set to work to get possession of the fat or blubber, which I knew would be very useful to us, but we found the task no pleasant one. Ernest and I cut several feet deep into the fat which covered the sides of the animal, while the others carried the masses of blubber we handed out to the boat; we literally swam in grease, for walls of solid fat rose on each side of us.

But we were not long the only claimants for the whale. A multitude of birds surrounded us. They flew round and round our heads, then, gradually approaching, they were so bold as to snatch pieces of fat from our hands. The birds were very troublesome, until I knocked down some with a club, and threw them into the boat. I took from the back of the animal a long band of skin, out of which I wanted to make a harness for the ass and the two buffaloes. It was a difficult task, the skin was so thick and so hard to cut; but I managed it after some difficulty. The tubs were placed in the canoe, and we set out along the coast with the new cargo we had acquired.

The next morning we again embarked in the canoe. A fresh wind was blowing, and we soon arrived at the island, which we found covered with gulls and other birds, who, in spite of the canvas with which the pieces that had been cut from the whale were covered, had made a plentiful meal.

We fired right and left into them before we could drive them away. Then, stripping off every article of clothing excepting our pantaloons, we set to work on our odious task. When at length evening came we abandoned the rest of our prey to the voracious birds; and, after having loaded our boat with a new cargo of whale blubber, we set sail for home.

In spite of our precautions our clothes stank of whale oil, and it was days before we could rid ourselves of the odour, yet we thought that what we had gained was worth a little personal inconvenience.

We had brought back with us some large flat pieces of whalebone, and with these I made a kind of paddle, which I fixed to the end of the boat. By turning a handle rapidly the flaps of whalebone beat the water, and answered the purpose of a propeller, so that we had no need to row. The boys were delighted with this new invention, and eager to make an excursion by boat.

This we did the first fine day, for the rains had now ceased. We coasted along and visited Falcon's Nest, and then went further to Prospect Hill, where we landed, and saw the animals we had left at the farm. The boat ran well, and the time taken was surprisingly short. We found all in order, though the sheep and goats had grown wild, and ran away when they saw us.

CHAPTER XXII

THE BOA CONSTRICTOR'S VISIT

ONE day, some time after, we were all sitting basket-making, an art we had recently learnt, when a shout from Fritz, who was generally on the alert, roused us.

'There is some large animal,' said he, 'coming in this direction. But it makes so much dust I can't see what it is.'

'Probably two or three sheep, or, perhaps, our sow, frolicking in the sand,' observed my wife.

'No, no,' replied Fritz, quickly, 'it is some curious animal. It rolls and unrolls itself alternately. I can see the rings of which it is formed. See, it is raising itself up, and looks like a huge mast in the dust. It advances — stops — marches on.'

I ran for the telescope, and directed it towards the object.

'I can see it plainly,' said Fritz, 'it has a greenish-coloured body.' 'What do you think of it?'

'That we must fly to the grotto,' I answered gravely.

'What do you think it is?'

'A serpent — a huge serpent, advancing directly towards us.'

'Shall I run for the guns?' he cried.

'No, no,' I answered, 'run all of you to the grotto. The serpent is too powerful to permit of our attacking him, unless we are ourselves in a place of safety.'

We hastened to gain the interior of the grotto, and prepared to receive our enemy. And we started none too soon, for he advanced so quickly, we had only just time to escape. When he reached the river bank we could see plainly that it was a huge boa constrictor, who writhed along towards us.

He crossed the bridge, and directed his course straight for the grotto. We had barricaded the door and the windows as well as we were able, and ascended into the dove-cot to which we had made an interior entrance. We passed our guns through the holes in the door, and waited silently.

The boa came on hesitatingly, until at last he stopped, about thirty yards in front of our position. Ernest, partly through nervousness, discharged his gun, and Jack and Francis followed his example.

The monster raised his head; but appeared to have received no wound. Fritz and I then fired, but without any effect, and the serpent glided away with inconceivable rapidity toward the marsh where our ducks and geese were, and disappeared in the rushes.

Exclamations accompanied his disappearance. Everyone was sure that they had hit him; but all agreed he was as yet unwounded. The boys chattered in a frenzy of excitement about his size and the colour of his scales.

I was in a state of great anxiety, for I could think of no way to rid ourselves of him. Meantime, I told everyone to remain in the grotto, and forbade them to open the door without my permission.

The fear of our terrible neighbour kept us shut up three days in our retreat — three long days of anguish and alarm.

The monster had given us no signs of his presence, and we would have supposed that he had gone, if the agitation among the ducks had not assured us of his presence. Every evening the whole colony made for the bay, and swam away to Whale Island, quacking loudly. Our food grew less and no outlet for escape presented itself.

The fodder that we happened to have in the grotto had also diminished; it was necessary to feed the cow, but I resolved to set the other animals at liberty to do for themselves. The donkey had grown very lively after his three days' rest and good food, and he no sooner saw a ray of light than he shot out of the door like an arrow, and was away in the open plain before we could stop him. It was a comical sight to see him kicking his heels in the air. But our mirth changed to horror when, suddenly, we saw the boa emerging from the rushes! He raised his head ten feet above the ground, darted out his forked tongue, and raced toward the donkey. The poor fellow saw his danger and began to run, braying with all his might; but neither his cries nor his legs could save him from his terrible enemy, and in a moment he was seized, enveloped, and crushed in the monstrous rings that the serpent threw around him.

We could hear his last bray, half stifled by the pressure of the boa, and then the cracking of his bones, for the boa, according to his nature, wound himself in great coils round his prey, and, in a few instants, crushed him to death. The monster, to give himself more power, had wound his tail about a piece of rock, which gave it the force of a lever, and we saw him kneading, like dough, the mass of flesh, among which we could distinguish nothing but the head. When the monster judged his preparation sufficient, he began to swallow the meal he had prepared. He placed before him the mass of flesh, and, extending his immense length along the ground, by a sudden effort distended his body frightfully; then, squirting a stream of saliva over the carcass, he began. Seizing the ass by the hind feet, by little and little we saw the whole body disappear. We observed that, as he advanced, the boa lost his strength; and, when all had been swallowed, he remained perfectly torpid and insensible.

The operation had been long: at seven o'clock it had begun, and at noon had just finished.

I saw that the time had arrived for action, and exclaiming, 'Now the boa is in our power!' I ran out from the grotto, carrying my loaded gun in my hand; Fritz followed close by my side; Jack came next, but the more timid Ernest lingered behind. I thought it best to pay no attention to him until all was over. Francis and his mother remained at home.

When we came near to him the boa raised his head, and, darting on me a look of powerless anger, again let it fall.

Fritz and I fired together, and both our shots entered the skull of the animal; but they did not produce death, and the eyes of the serpent sparkled with rage. We advanced nearer, and, firing our pistols directly through the eye, we saw his rings contract, a slight quiver ran through his body, and he lay dead upon the sand before us, stretched out like the mast of a ship.

We set up a shout of victory, and we huzzaed so long and loud, that Ernest, Francis, and my wife came running down toward us.

After the three days that we had spent in the grotto, we felt the pleasure of being free again; it was a second deliverance, almost as great as that from our shipwreck.

As I thought it best to finish immediately with the boa, I sent Fritz and Jack to the grotto, with injunctions to bring back the buffalo. I remained with Ernest and Francis, to keep off the birds of prey, which already hovered round the carcass, for I wished to preserve the brilliant-coloured skin with which it was covered.

I told Ernest meantime to make a verse that would do as an epitaph for our poor donkey, and after a few minutes thought he produced the following lines:

'Here rests a faithful ass,
   Who his master once disobey'd,
And was devour'd by a snake at last,
   Who of him a breakfast made.'

'Wonderful! wonderful!' cried I, and drawing a piece of red lead from my pocket, I scrawled the verses, at his dictation, on the surface of the rock.

I had scarcely finished when Fritz and his brother returned with the buffalo, and burst out laughing derisively at the effusion.

We began our work by attaching the buffalo to the head of the donkey, which yet projected from the mouth of the boa. While we held the serpent by the tail, he pulled from its stomach the disfigured remains of our unfortunate donkey. We buried him in the earth near by, and piled some pieces of rock over him for a monument.

The buffalo was then attached to the tail of the monster, and we set out for the grotto, supporting the head to prevent it from trailing on the ground.

'How shall we go to work to get the skin off?' asked the boys, as we deposited our heavy burden before the grotto.

'See if you cannot find a way yourselves,' said I, good-humouredly.

'I have thought of a simple method,' cried Ernest; 'one I have often seen employed to skin eels, and which will do for the boa too. It is this; to cut the skin around the neck, and, loosening the first part, attach strong cords to it, fasten the cord to the buffalo, and, taking care to secure the head of the serpent strongly, drive the animal in the opposite direction, and by that means draw off the whole skin.'

'Very well,' I assented; 'to the work. I leave the whole labour and the honour of the invention to you alone. As for the preparation of the skin, nothing can be easier: after you have cleaned the head as well as possible, you can wash the skin with salt water, sand, and ashes; then you must expose it to the sun's rays to dry, and, finally, fill it with hay, cotton, and all sorts of light materials.'

Fritz assured me that he understood all that I wished done, but that he was afraid they would not succeed.

So they began. And when at length they got it off, the skin was washed, dried, and prepared as I had directed; and I could not help laughing to see the strange method they adopted in stuffing it. They hoisted the snake up to the branch of a tree, and Jack, in his swimming costume, jumped into the long hollow skin, and trampled down the hay, moss, and cotton that his brothers threw to him with their pitchforks. When the skin was full, we saw him sticking his head out of the hole, and hurrahing with all his might.

When this work, which had occupied a whole day, was finished, we mended the holes that our shot had made in the skin; and, with a piece of cochineal, gave to the tongue that blood-red colour of which death had deprived it; then we elevated it on a wooden stand, arranging its body as gracefully as possible around the pole, and fixing the jaws half open. Our dogs began to bark as soon as they saw it: and our animals recoiled from it as if it were a living boa. So arranged, it was solemnly installed in our library, where it took the first rank among our curiosities; at the same time Ernest wrote over the door the following legend: 'Asses cannot enter here.'

We had nothing more to fear from the boa; but I was afraid it might have either left its mate behind it, or else a nest of little ones, which in time would spread terror through the land. I resolved in consequence to undertake two expeditions — the one through the marsh, the other toward Falcon's Nest, through the passage in the rock, whence I supposed the boa had come. Ernest and Jack begged me to allow them to stay at home, for even the usually fearless Jack was nervous.

'I shiver with fright,' said he, 'to think of meeting one of those horrible serpents in the rushes.'

I endeavoured to overcome this childishness, and he succeeded in calming himself, and came with us.

We set out loaded with our guns. We carried some boards, and the bladders of sea-dogs, to sustain us on the water if necessary. The boards we wanted for use in the marsh, for by placing one before the other, and taking them up, we could walk over the quagmire. We easily recognised the traces of the boa; the rushes were bent down where he had passed through, and there were deep spiral impressions in the wet ground where he had rested his enormous rings. But we discovered nothing to make us believe that he had had a companion: we found neither eggs nor little ones — nothing but a nest of dried rushes, and I did not think that the boa had constructed even that. Arrived at the end of the marsh, we made an interesting discovery; it was that of a new grotto, which opened out of the rock, and from this flowed a little stream that passed on among the rushes of the marsh.

The floor was composed of an extremely fine and white sort of earth, which, after examining it, I recognised as being 'fullers' clay.' I immediately gathered some handfuls, and carefully placed them in my pocket-handkerchief.

'Here,' said I to the boys, who were regarding me with astonishment, 'is a discovery that will be very welcome to your mother, for this is what soap is made of.'

'I thought,' said Ernest, ' that soap was made by men.'

'The soap that is ordinarily used is made of all sorts of things,' I answered, 'but there is nothing so good as this.'

As we came out of the grotto Jack, who had stayed behind in the marsh, shouted to us that he had killed a young boa. When we came to examine it, however, we found it was only a large eel, which brought forth a shout of laughter from his brothers.

However, I praised him for his pluck, though his enemy had not been so dangerous as he imagined. When we returned home I presented to my wife the 'fullers' clay,' and told her the adventures and discoveries of the day.

CHAPTER XXIII

OSTRICHES IN THE DESERT

HOWEVER, I was not altogether satisfied that another boa might not be lurking in the woods, and I determined to go as far as possible throughout our whole domain to set our fears at rest. We stayed a day or two at Falcon's Nest to put things straight, and then passed on to Prospect Hill. We found nothing to alarm us on the way, and at the farm our livestock seemed very prosperous. Having stayed here a night, we decided to go on further the next day, and to explore what still remained unknown to us of the island.

We began our march at daylight, and, after having journeyed on for about two hours, I gave the signal for a halt. We had arrived at a pleasant spot, which commanded a far-reaching prospect, and was defended, on one side, by a thick pine forest, and on the other by the narrow defile through which Jack and I had once before passed.

'Here,' said Fritz, 'we can defend ourselves against all enemies, and, if you take my advice, father, you will establish a post here.'

Jack, who never attended to the conversation of those around him, caught at the last words his brother had spoken, and bellowed out:

'A post-office! Why, where can we send the letters to?'

'Australia and New Zealand,' replied I, as gravely as possible, whereat there was a general laugh.

The rest of the morning was devoted to the fortification of our camp. We then dined; but the heat was so powerful that we were obliged to postpone any extra labour until the next day.

Nothing troubled the repose of the night. We were up at daylight, and in a few moments our preparations for a further exploration were complete. I took with me my three eldest sons, leaving Francis with his mother.

We passed through the defile, and ventured into a country where we had been but once before. Jack recognised the place where we had taken the buffalo. The river, which divided the plain, was bordered by a rich line of vegetation. We followed its course for some time; but as we advanced, vegetation disappeared, and we soon found ourselves in the middle of an immense plain, only bounded by the horizon. The sun beat right down on our heads, the sand burned our feet — in one word, it was a desert — a desert without a single tree — a desert of sand, the only green things being a few withered geraniums, and some sort of grass that contrasted strangely with the aridity of the soil. On crossing the river, we had filled our gourds with fresh water, but the sun had heated it so that we could not drink it, and we were obliged to throw it away.

After two hours of painful journeying we arrived at the foot of the hill, that we had perceived afar off. It was a rock that gave us some shade, and afforded us a refuge against the rays of the sun. We were too fatigued to climb the rock and reconnoitre the country; we could scarcely stand against the overpowering rays of the sun, and our dogs were as tired as ourselves; we were isolated in the middle of the desert, though we could see the river in the distance.

We had scarcely been seated five minutes when Nip, who had accompanied us, suddenly disappeared over the rock, having probably scented some brother monkeys in the neighbourhood; our dogs also deserted us; but we were too tired to call them back.

I brought out some morsels of sugar-cane, and distributed them among the boys, for our thirst was terrible. This refreshment restored our appetites, and some rounds of roast peccary revived our spirits.

Suddenly Fritz cried out:

'There are two horsemen galloping up towards us. There, a third has joined them — perhaps they are Arabs of the desert.'

I exclaimed with astonishment, and produced the telescope. Fritz, whose sight was the best, took it.

'Oh, I see now a number of waggons loaded with hay; but they are so distant I can scarcely distinguish anything,' he cried.

'Let me have the glass,' cried Jack, impatiently; and he declared he saw a crowd of cavaliers who carried little lances, with banners at the point.

'Come, give me the glass now,' said I; and, after having looked some time attentively:

'Well,' said I to Jack, ' your Arabs, your cavaliers with lances, your hay-carts, what do you think they have been transformed into?'

'Camelopards, perhaps ?'

'No; although not a bad idea, yet they are ostriches, and chance has thrown a splendid chase into our hands.'

'Ostriches!' cried Jack and Fritz: 'how grand!'

'However can we catch them?' cried Ernest.

The ostriches were rapidly approaching; I ordered Fritz and Jack to go in search of the dogs, whilst Ernest and I sought some shelter where we could hide. We threw ourselves down behind some large tufts of a plant that grew among the rocks.

Jack and Fritz now returned with the dogs, who, from their wet coats, had evidently been taking a bath somewhere.

The ostriches were now within eyesight, and I could distinguish three females and a male, the last easily recognised by the long white feathers of his tail. We crouched closer to the ground, and held our dogs close to our sides.

Luckily Fritz had brought his eagle, who was now trained to do the work required of him, and I began to see that our success would depend on his obedience. I told Fritz to hold him in readiness in case he should be needed.

The ostriches soon became aware of our presence — they appeared to hesitate in their march; but, as we remained immovable, they at last seemed reassured, and were advancing directly to us, when our dogs, whom we could not keep quiet, suddenly sprang out upon them. Away went the timid birds, with a rapidity that can be compared to nothing else but the wind driving before it a bundle of feathers. Their feet did not appear to touch the ground, their half-extended wings had the appearance of sails, and the swiftest horse could not have overtaken them. I ordered Fritz to unhood his eagle; he did so, and the noble bird soon lit upon the head of the male ostrich, and, attacking his eyes, brought him to the ground. The dogs ran up, and when we arrived the bird was just dying under the wounds that the animals had inflicted.

We were greatly disappointed at this, but we could not have helped it, and we looked with pity at the magnificent bird extended before us. We took some of the white plumes from his tail, so that we could decorate our hats with them.

'What a pity,' said Fritz, as we examined the gigantic proportions of our victim, 'to kill such a fine bird. We might have tamed it. and taught it to know us.'

Jack and Ernest meantime had wandered away, and we now saw them waving their plumed hats in the air, and shouting to us to hurry.

'A nest!' they cried, 'an ostrich's nest! Quick — quick!'

We found the two boys standing over a large ostrich-nest — if we can dignify a hole dug in the ground by the name of nest — in which were arranged from twenty-five to thirty eggs, each as large as a child's head.

'Take care,' I said to them, 'don't touch them, for if you do the female will desert her nest.'

However, the boys were so eager to take some home, I allowed each of them to choose one, leaving the rest untouched. They soon repented of their wish, for the eggs were heavy, and they changed their burden from hand to hand, with all the signs of fatigue. I came to their assistance, and advised them to cut some branches from a low sort of pine that grew about the rocks, and make a basket in which to carry their eggs.

My plan succeeded admirably, and the boys began their march without the slightest complaint.

We then arrived at the borders of a swamp; here we could trace the marks of the dogs and the monkey, and recognised this as the place where they had wet themselves. We could see in the distance troops of buffaloes, monkeys, and antelopes, but so far from us that we took no further notice of them; nothing, however, indicated to us the presence of a boa.

We halted at this marsh, and refreshed ourselves with a drink, then filling our gourds with water, prepared to depart, when we made a discovery. I saw a round object resembling a mass of moist earth, and when I threw it into the water to clean it, what was my astonishment to see it move! I took it out, and, on examining it, discovered it to be a turtle of the smallest kind, scarcely as large as an apple.

We soon noticed a dozen of the little turtles crawling around us, some of which I picked up and put in my knapsack.

CHAPTER XXIV

BEARS! BEARS!

THEN we quitted the borders of the swamp, and followed a little stream of water that led us to a rock. We found trees, grass — in short, a little oasis in the desert, and we named it 'Green Valley.' We soon, however, left its verdure far behind us, and again we were in the desert; but the heat was not as violent as it had been, so we journeyed tranquilly on, carrying our ostrich-eggs.

We were yet distant about half an hour's journey from the large cave. Jack and Fritz had stopped a moment to adjust their burdens, and I stopped with them, while Ernest had marched forward.

'The philosopher is in a hurry to get home,' said Jack, laughing, 'he runs that he may be rested first.'

But scarcely had he finished his sentence, when we heard a cry of distress from Ernest, followed by two terrible howls, mingled with the barking of the dogs. A moment after, the boy reappeared; he was running at full speed, his face deadly pale, and he cried out in a voice stifled with fear:

'Bears! bears! they are following me,' and fell into my arms more dead than alive. I had not time to reassure him, and I felt myself seized with a sudden shiver, as an enormous bear appeared, immediately followed by a second.

'Courage, boys,' was all I could say. I seized my gun, and prepared to receive the enemy. Fritz did the same, and, with a courage and coolness far above his years, he took his place by my side. Jack also took his gun, but remained in the rear, while Ernest, who had no arms — for in his fright he had let his gun fall — took to his heels and ran away.

But our dogs had already flown at the bears. We fired together, and, although our shots did not bring down the enemy, they nevertheless told well. One of the bears had a jaw broken, the other a shoulder fractured. Our faithful dogs did prodigies of valour. They fought most desperately, rolling in the dust with their enemies. We would have fired again, but we were afraid that we should kill the dogs. So we advanced nearer, and, at about four paces from the bears, we discharged our pistols directly at their heads. The huge animals gave a groan, and then fell back motionless on the sand.

We remained some time dumb with astonishment. Our dogs, covered with wounds, were still tearing the bears as if they were alive. Jack was the first to sing out victory, and he brought back poor Ernest, who still trembled all over. I asked him how he had come across the bears. He answered, with tears in his eyes, that he had run on before us in order to frighten Jack, by imitating the growling of bears, and his terror when he found his jest transformed into a reality was overwhelming.

The moral was so obvious that I did not call attention to it. A minute's silence followed, then Jack remarked that the presence of bears in a country so warm was rather extraordinary.

'I cannot explain it to you,' said I.

During this time the boys had approached the two animals. They passed their hands over the long line of sharp teeth, with which their jaws were furnished, raised their huge paws armed with terrible claws, and admired their shaggy coats.

We took the precaution before leaving, to draw the two carcasses into the cave, and cover them with thorn bushes, to keep off all carnivorous beasts and birds of prey. We also buried our ostrich-eggs in the sand, so that we might fetch them the next day.

The sun was set when we rejoined the others. A good fire and a well-cooked supper awaited us. My wife was so frightened at the account of the bears, that she could not restrain her tears; and, although I assured her that the flesh of the bears would make capital meat, and was well worth having, she begged me not to return into the desert.

We lighted a large fire to guard us through the night, and our dogs, whose wounds my wife had washed and dressed, lay down beside it. The next morning it required a strong effort to tear us from our beds, so wearied out had we been the preceding day. We breakfasted in haste. The beasts were harnessed to the cart, and, after a pleasant little run, we arrived safe and sound at the cavern of the bears.

On approaching, we found the entrance of the cave filled by a troop of birds, whom, by their ruffled necks and the colour of their feathers, we should have taken to be turkey cocks, if a nearer examination had not convinced us that they were birds of prey, as we could see them flying out carrying away huge pieces of the flesh. I thought, by the immense number of birds, that our work was finished, and nothing would be left but the bones, when suddenly we heard a flapping of wings above us, and a black shadow passed along the ground. We raised our eyes, and beheld a bird of prodigious size, whose wings extended full sixteen feet. As he came gradually sweeping down toward us, Fritz fired his gun and the formidable creature fell dead at our feet. It had been shot in the heart.

The report of the gun had frightened the band of marauders, and they flew away stunning our ears with the horrible discord that they made. We then entered the cavern, and found one of the bears half devoured, and the other partly so. We loaded our cart with the skins and the remaining meat, and placing the immense bird, which we had discovered to be a condor of the largest size, upon the top, we set off for the camp.

We devoted a whole day to the preparation of the bears' flesh. After having skinned the animals with the utmost care and precaution, I cut off the hams, and then divided the rest of the meat into long strips, about an inch in thickness, and these we exposed, with the hams, to a good current of smoke. The grease was collected in bamboo canes, and carefully preserved; for, besides its use in the kitchen, my wife said it was excellent on bread instead of butter. We left the carcasses to our dogs, and they, aided by the birds of prey, soon picked the bones so clean, that there remained nothing but two perfectly white, dry skeletons, which we carried home with us for our museum. As for the skins, they were carefully washed with salt water, and rubbed with sand and ashes in order to render them soft.

Our labours had been too peaceful for the restless boys, and the next morning I proposed to them to make an excursion alone in the desert; my proposition was joyfully received. Ernest refused to go, but Fritz, Jack, and Francis were soon in the saddle, and galloped off through the defile.

There was plenty for us who remained at home to occupy ourselves with, among other things, while examining a small cavern which we had discovered near the tent, I found a block of talc, nearly as transparent as glass, which I resolved to make into window-panes.

It is not difficult to split this material into very thin sheets, and though not so clear as glass, it answers the purpose very well.

As evening approached we gathered around our hearth, where my wife was cooking two bear's paws, which had been well soaked in brine, and the smell of which promised us a capital supper. Not long after the galloping of steeds was heard, and in another moment the boys were at our side.

Jack and Francis each carried a little kid on his back, with the feet tied together, and Fritz's game-bag appeared to me to be pretty full.

'A fine chase, papa!' cried Jack. 'Storm' — for so he had named his buffalo — 'carried me through the desert like a flash of lightning. Fritz has two Angora rabbits in his pouch, and also a cuckoo, who led us to one of the finest hives I have ever seen; we shall be able to get plenty of honey.'

'Jack has not told all,' said Fritz. 'We have taken a whole troop of antelopes prisoners, and have driven them into our domains, where we can hunt them and tame them just when we please.'

He then went on eagerly to tell me that, having spied the herd of antelopes, they had cautiously driven them into a defile, across the mouth of which they had stretched a long string, to which they had attached their handkerchiefs, ostrich feathers, and everything else they could think of to prevent the animals re-passing.

'My turn!' cried Jack, when Fritz had stopped for breath. 'His eagle swooped down on two rabbits, which we rescued before he had hurt them. Then we heard a cuckoo, which flew on before us until it stopped over a bee's nest. Armed with some sulphur matches that I found in my knapsack, I advanced and tried to suffocate the bees by throwing the lighted matches down the hole, when suddenly a rumbling noise was heard, and, in a second, a swarm of bees emerged, attacking me on all sides.

'I could scarcely believe,' said Jack, as he finished his recital, 'that so small a creature could cause so much pain, but I ought to have known, for it is not my first experience.'

I had noticed while he was speaking that his face was red and inflamed, but I had not had time to get a word in edgeways. Now I told him to go to his mother, and let her put something on his face to allay the pain.

I then made a basket of willows, covered with canvas at the top, in which to put the rabbits and the kids, so that they might be easily carried to Cliff House, as we had named our new residence in the grotto. We were undetermined whether we would keep them there, or leave them on one of the islands of the coast.

Soon came the welcome call to supper. The bear's paws formed the principal dish; and we found it was one of the most delicate we had ever eaten, and my wife was loaded with praises for her good cookery. After supper we lighted our torches and fires, and lay down to enjoy our night's rest.

CHAPTER XXV

RIDING ON AN OSTRICH

I WISHED to make another excursion into the desert before returning home, to get some more ostrich-eggs. Fritz gave up his wild ass to me, and took the young colt, and Jack and Francis each mounted their respective beasts. Ernest preferred to remain at home; he had succeeded Francis as assistant in the kitchen.

We took the dogs with us, and accomplished the first part of the journey without incident.

We had scarcely come in sight of the nest when we saw four ostriches rise from the sand and advance toward us. Fritz's first care was to prepare his eagle for the conflict by muzzling it, so that it could not strike the ostrich's eyes as before. On the huge birds came, with half-extended wings, gliding over the ground with inconceivable rapidity. They seemed to think us inanimate objects, for they made directly for us until they had arrived within pistol-shot; there were three females and a male — the last a little in advance, with his beautiful tailfeathers floating behind him. The moment of attack was come. I seized my string with balls, and, calling up all my sleight-of-hand, I launched it against the male ostrich. Unfortunately, however, instead of catching him around the legs, as I intended, the balls of my string took a turn round his body, and I only fastened his wings to his sides. It diminished his speed somewhat, but the frightened bird turned round, and, using his long legs, endeavoured to escape. Away we dashed after him, I on the ass and Fritz on the colt. But we were nearly exhausted, when, happily, Jack and Francis rode up and cut off his farther retreat.

Fritz then unhooded his eagle, and, pointing out the ostrich to him, it immediately pounced upon its prey. And now commenced an arduous chase. Jack and Francis on one side, and Fritz and I on the other, tormented him and harassed him without ceasing; but the most useful combatant was the eagle. The presence of this new enemy troubled the ostrich greatly; he felt him on his head, and heard the flapping of his wings, while, on the other hand, the eagle, furious at finding his beak strongly fastened by cotton, was so violent that, by a vigorous stroke of his wings, he fairly felled the ostrich.

A cry of joy burst from the huntsmen, and Jack, throwing his balls, caught the bird round the legs, and sent him helpless to the ground at the very moment he was about to recover and bound off. He was very violent, and struggled so vigorously that I hardly dared to approach him. But imagining that, by depriving him of light, I might reduce his fury, I threw my vest and handkerchief over his head. I had discovered the secret. No sooner were his eyes covered than he became as quiet as a lamb. I approached, passed a large band of sea-dog-skin around his body, two other bands were attached as reins to each side, and his legs were fastened with strong cords, long enough to allow him to walk, but confining him sufficiently to prevent his escape.

'A fine prize, truly!' said Jack, when our work was done. 'We have got the giant, but how shall we tame him?'

'I thought of that before,' replied I. 'We might fasten him between the bull and the buffalo, for example, and you two, each armed with a whip, could teach him to march in a line with them.'

'Oh, that would be fine fun!' they cried.

I accordingly attached our two coursers before and behind the ostrich with strong cords, and, when all was ready, my two cavaliers jumped into their saddles, and I pulled the covering from the head of the ostrich.

The bird remained some time immovable, as if astonished at the return of light. It soon made a start, but the ropes pulled it roughly back, and it fell down on its knees; again it made the attempt, and again it was foiled. It tried to fly, but its wings were tightly fastened by the band I had passed around them; its legs were also restrained. It threw itself from side to side with the utmost violence, but the patient buffaloes did not pay the least attention to the pulling and hauling. At last the bird appeared convinced of the inutility of its efforts, and, submitting to its two companions, set off with them at full gallop. They dashed gallantly on for half an hour, until the buffalo and the bull, less accustomed to the sands of the savanna than the ostrich, forced it to abate its rapid pace, and adopt a slower movement.

While this was going on, Fritz and I set out in search of the ostrich-nest. As we approached, a female bird rose up off the nest and fled rapidly away into the desert. I had taken care to bring with me a sack and a quantity of cotton. I now took out six of the eggs, and, enveloping them as carefully as possible in the cotton, placed them in the sack, leaving the others in the nest, in hopes the mother would not discover the theft. The sack containing the eggs was carefully fastened on the back of the ass, whom I led slowly along, while Fritz mounted his colt.

We soon arrived at the tent, where Ernest and his mother received us with an astonishment they could not find words to express.

'What, in the name of patience,' cried my wife, as she perceived the ostrich, 'are you going to do with that immense bird?'

'A post-horse, mamma,' cried Jack — 'a posthorse that I mean to name "Hurricane," for nothing else can run so fast. Nobody else shall ride him but me, and I will give you Storm, Ernest, because you have no mount.'

On hearing this Francis cried out that the ostrich belonged to him as much as to Jack.

'Very well,' said I, 'let us divide him. Fritz, you may take the head, for it was your eagle that stunned him; I claim the body, for it was my string and balls that caught that; Jack, you own the legs your balls captured them; and we will give you, Francis, a feather from the tail, as it was there, I believe, you kicked the bird to make it stand up.'

At this they all laughed, and the question was left undecided.

I fastened the ostrich securely between two trees, where I left him for the night.

The next day we set off early. The ostrich took his place between the bull and the buffalo, as before. He was at first inclined to be refractory, and threw himself from right to left, but all in vain; his two conductors were like immovable masses, against which all resistance was unavailing.

Fritz mounted the young colt Rapid, and I the ass, while Ernest drove the cart, in which sat my wife.

We halted at the entrance of the defile where my sons had suspended the cord with the feathers attached, to keep back the antelopes and gazelles. In the place of the cord we erected a solid palisade of bamboo, high enough to keep out all animals that do not climb.

Our labours detained us a long time, and it was night when we arrived at the cabin of the farm. We lighted a fire, and after supper extended ourselves on our sacks of cotton and went to sleep.

The next day we discovered a new treasure: our hen-house had received an addition of twenty chickens, the product of some eggs Jack had brought home in his hat.

It was long after noon when our weary journey was finished and we once more arrived at Cliff House. We were worn out with fatigue; the sun's rays had been pouring down on our heads all day, and our strength was so exhausted we could scarcely give our animals their evening food.

The day after our arrival my wife began a 'spring cleaning.' Windows were opened, beds aired, and all swept and garnished.

We had tied the ostrich at first under a tree, and securely fastened his feet; but we changed his situation, and now tied him to one of the strong bamboo columns that supported the gallery.

We next looked at the eggs, and tried them with warm water to see if we could still hatch them. I found that a few had life in them, so I constructed an oven, in which I placed them as if it were an incubator.

We then installed our Angora rabbits on Shark Island, after constructing a burrow in the ground, similar to those of Europe. Before putting them in, we combed them, and removed all the superfluous hair, which I intended to manufacture into hats.

Then we turned to the education of the ostrich, which was more difficult than anything we had yet attempted.

He began by flying into a terrible passion; he struggled, snapped at us with his beak, and cut all sorts of capers; and we could find no better remedy for such conduct than to treat him as we had treated Fritz's eagle — that was, by burning tobacco under his nose. This had the desired effect, and we soon saw the majestic bird totter and fall insensible to the ground. We had recourse to this plan several times. Little by little we relaxed the cord which fastened the bird to the bamboo post, and gave him room to wander about the doorway. A litter of rushes was provided for him; calabashes filled with sweet nuts, rice, maize, and guavas were placed every day before him.

During three days all our cares were in vain: the beautiful captive would not eat, and he carried his obstinacy so far that I was seriously afraid of the consequences. At last an idea occurred to us. It was to poke down the throat of the bird, willy nilly, balls of maize and butter. The ostrich made horrible faces at first, but when he tasted the balls, all trouble on that point was over, and the delicacies we placed before him were quickly devoured, the guavas being especially favoured.

The natural savageness of the ostrich disappeared more and more every day; he would let us approach him without striking at us, and

104

after some days we thought we could, without much risk, unfasten him to take a short lesson in the art of walking. We placed him between the buffalo and the bull, and put him through all the exercises of the stable to trot, to gallop, stop short, trot again, walk, etc. I cannot say that the poor bird relished his first lesson very much, but the tobacco pipe and the whip were two admirable instructors, and when he was disposed to become unruly a whiff of tobacco would set all to rights.

At the end of the month his education was complete. The next thing to be thought of was a bit; but how could I contrive a bit for a beak? I had remarked, however, that the absence of light had a very direct influence upon the ostrich; he would stop short when blindfold, and could not be induced to move until his eyes were uncovered. So I made, with the skin of a sea-dog, a sort of hood, which covered the head, being fastened about the neck. I made two openings in the side of this hood, one opposite each eye, and I covered each of these holes with one of our little turtle-shells, attached to a whale-bone spring, fixed in such a manner that it would open and shut. Reins were fastened to these eye-caps, so that we could open or shut them, just as we pleased. When the two shells were open, the ostrich galloped straight on; when one was opened he went in a direction corresponding with the eye that received light, and when both shells were shut, he would stop short. The most fully trained horse could not have obeyed better than our ostrich did, under his novel head-dress.

The next thing was to teach him to carry someone on his back, but we had a great deal of difficulty in making him submit to our wishes. I was not, however, discouraged, and at last we had the satisfaction of seeing our new courser striding swiftly along with one of the boys on his back.

After this the question of ownership came up again, with all its difficulties. Jack would not give up his pretensions, while Francis and Fritz protested loudly against his rights.

Jack was lighter and more agile than his two elder brothers; on the other hand he was stronger than Francis. These two considerations decided the matter in his favour, and he was adjudged to be the owner of the animal, but on one condition: that everybody should be allowed to ride him, and that he should be more generally recognised as common property than the other animals.

This decision gave Jack much joy, and he readily agreed to the conditions.

Out of the six ostrich eggs, which we had put in the incubator,

105

three had hatched. The young ostriches were the drollest looking animals that could be imagined. They were like ducks, mounted on long legs, and they tottered awkwardly about on their slender stilts. One died the day after its birth, and we fed the others on maize, acorns, boiled rice, milk, and cassava bread.

Our next care was to cure our bear skins, which we had hitherto left in running water. I carefully removed all particles of flesh that adhered to them, rubbed them with vinegar several times, and then, with a mixture of ashes and grease, worked at them constantly until they had attained the desired softness, and we thus obtained two superb, warm coverings.

When all our provisions were gathered in, and we felt sure that we could get through the winter without being starved, we began our manufacture of hats.

I cut a wooden head, which we divided into two parts, and on which we spread a thick layer of soft paste, composed of rat skin and the glue of fishes. We let it dry, and as it took the exact impress of the mould, we obtained a sort of cap.

'Is it a hat, a bonnet, or a cap?' asked Ernest, laughing.

'Hat or cap,' said Fritz, 'it is of a most abominable colour, and I vote that it should be dyed.'

'Yes,' replied Ernest; 'Let it be red, it's the poet's colour.'

Francis preferred grey, Jack green, as being the favourite colour of the hunter, while Fritz — the prudent Fritz — voted for white, as he had read that this attracted less heat than any colour.

'Fritz's choice showed his judgment,' I said, 'Jack picked out his more for ornament than use; and as for Ernest, his it must be, as it is the only one I can manage.'

I turned to the cochineal, and soon gave the hat a brilliant red tint. I adorned it with a couple of ostrich plumes, and my wife passed a ribbon round it. Then I handed it to Francis, who had lost his cap the day before.

Francis was a beautiful child, and he looked very handsome in it. His auburn curls fell over his forehead, and his fair complexion shone out beneath the rich red hat. His brothers looked at him with envy, and clamoured for a similar adornment.

But materials were wanting, and I engaged my boys to procure as many rat skins as possible. I began by making a lot of rat traps, similar to those used in Europe, and armed with these, we set off for the resort of the rats.

For bait I employed a sort of little fish that we found in abundance in the marsh, and which the rats appeared very fond of. My traps succeeded, and we returned to the grotto with an ample supply of rat skins.

Our hat-manufacturing occupied us about ten days, and we were very successful.

CHAPTER XXVI

THE BOYS' EXCURSION

As Francis grew older his adventurous spirit showed itself in his desire to accompany his brothers everywhere, while Ernest was only too glad to stay at home with his mother and me. One day Fritz, Jack, and Francis had thus gone off together, and towards evening, when we began to grow anxious about their return, Jack appeared in the distance. He arrived at a great pace on his ostrich, having left his brothers far behind. He brought nothing with him, pretending that his courser would receive no other burden than himself. Fritz and Francis followed him, and each carried before him a sack full of game, the products of the chase, in which they had been extremely fortunate; they had brought back with them four strange beasts whom they had christened 'beasts with a bill,' one monkey, a kangaroo, and two varieties of the musk-rat, which they had found in the swamp.

The boys were very hungry, and we had an admirable supper ready for them. First came roast pork. By the side of the pig was placed a plate of nice fresh salad; opposite to that was a dish of jelly; for dessert we had a sort of fritters made from guava apples; sweetmeats, of cinnamon preserved in sugar; and these were all set out with as much precision and nicety as if we had been in Europe, instead of on a desert island.

They breathlessly related their adventures, supplementing and contradicting one another freely during the meal, and ended by begging me to skin the kangaroo. I invented for that purpose a machine, which caused a great deal of laughter among the boys.

We had found on board the ship, in the surgeon's case of instruments, a large syringe. Without saying anything concerning it to my sons, who stood watching me with astonishment, I ordered them to

107

suspend the kangaroo by the hind legs, at such a height that the breast of the animal would be about level with mine. When this preparatory arrangement was concluded I made an incision in the skin, and then took hold of my syringe. I introduced the end of the syringe into the incision I had made in the skin, and worked the instrument. By little and little the skin of the animal became inflated, and soon it was but a shapeless mass.

'To work, to work!' cried I to the astonished boys; 'beat this blown-up skin with your sticks, and you will soon have it off.'

And really, after having made an incision the length of the stomach, the skin peeled off easily.

I explained to them that the skins of some animals are only fastened to the flesh by a tissue of extremely tender and delicate fibres. By means of the syringe I had injected between the flesh and the skin a certain amount of air, which, distending the skin, broke loose the small fibres, and thus rendered the skinning of the animal a very easy operation.

They were much interested, and, I could see, looked upon me almost as a magician for having thought of such a thing.

The next large operation that claimed our attention was to gather in and thresh the corn we had sown, which had now sprung up to a good harvest.

We prepared a hard, dry floor of trodden earth, and threw upon it the heads of the corn, which we cut off in bunches and conveyed to the scene of action in baskets. Then I told my three horsemen to mount and ride their steeds up and down until their feet had trodden the grain from the husk. It was a curious sight.

The bull, the ass, and the ostrich rivalled each other in swiftness. My wife, Ernest, and I, each armed with a pitchfork, followed after them, throwing the grain under the feet of the animals.

When the grain was all threshed, we set to work to clear it of the straws and dirt that had become mixed with it. This was the most difficult and painful part of all the labour. But when we had finished, we found we had sixty bushels of barley, eighty of wheat, and more than a hundred of maize — enough, at all events, to insure us against a flour famine.

When the land was all cleared I sowed it again, but, in order not to exhaust the soil, I sowed wheat and oats.

108

CHAPTER XXVII

FRITZ AND HIS CAJACK

THE rainy season was now rapidly approaching, and we were soon obliged to give up our excursions. The winds and the rain commenced; the sky that had so long been clear became dark with storm clouds; tempests announced the approach of winter; and we closed the door of our grotto, happy in having such a comfortable shelter.

The turning-wheel was continually in motion. We improved the quality of our manufactures more and more, and we made utensils that at the outset we had despaired of ever possessing.

Of all the instruments at our disposal, the English turning-lathe was the most serviceable, and my wife made such frequent appeals to its powers that she finished by making me a capital workman.

Ernest found occupation enough in his books; but his brothers never entered the library unless driven by necessity. I felt the urgency of providing some active occupation for them, and Fritz came to my assistance.

He suggested that we should make a light canoe, or cajack, as the Greenlanders call it, suitable for one person.

The Greenlanders make theirs of walrus-skin, but we had none of this, and I thought, perhaps, the skin of dog-fish, of which we had plenty, might do as well, so I caught at the suggestion.

Strips of whalebone, bamboo-cane, and rushes, with some dog-fish skin, were accordingly the materials that we employed. Two arched strips of whalebone fastened at each end, and separated in the middle by a piece of bamboo fixed transversely across, formed the two sides of our canoe; other pieces of whalebone, woven in with rushes and moss, well covered with pitch, formed the skeleton. The first improvement on the cajack, was to arrange it so that the rower could sit; while, in the cajacks of the Greenlander, he is obliged to remain with the legs crossed, like a tailor, or else to lie down in the bottom of the boat.

This boat of osiers, whalebone, and bamboo, was, when finished, so light and elastic, that it would rebound like a ball from the earth; and when we put it in the water, although heavily laden, it scarcely drew two inches. We were engaged upon our new work more than a month; but it succeeded so well that my sons were delighted with it.

When the skeleton was finished, and the interior covered with a coat of gum and moss, we began to make an envelope. For this I took the two entire skins of sea-calves, fastened one at each end of the canoe, and then drew them down under it, where they were strongly sewed together, and covered with a gum elastic coat, to render them impervious to water. Next I made oars of bamboo, and fastened bladders to one end, so that they might be useful in case of accident. I also constructed in the bow a place to receive a sail.

Fritz, whose idea it was, was pronounced owner of the cajack, Jack and Ernest being but little tempted by so seemingly dangerous a construction.

My wife, in order to take her part, made a complete swimming costume for Fritz.

A jacket of the skin of the whale's entrails, hermetically sealed and sewed round the borders, so that the air could not possibly escape, was furnished with a flexible pipe, closed with a valve, so that it could be inflated or exhausted at the pleasure of its wearer. Thus, if any accident did happen to him, he would be comparatively safe.

The winter had glided away; reading, the study of languages, and other literary pursuits had been mingled with our domestic occupations, and helped to make the gloomy days pass.

The wind calmed, the sea resumed its smoothness the grass sprang up under our feet, and we revisited Falcon's Nest, with its giant trees and its rich harvest of springing grain.

The swimming costume was the last thing that we had made, and Fritz was anxious to try it; consequently, one fine afternoon, dinner over, he put on his jacket, which was drawn close round his neck; then his hood, with its pipe for air, was fitted to the jacket, and two pieces of talc inserted so that he could see. He looked so droll that we all burst into a fit of laughter; but he plunged gravely into the water, and struck out for Shark Island.

When he returned we found that his costume was quite water-tight, and he might safely brave a wetting anywhere.

The trial of the cajack was a grand holiday fête. All were anxious to join in it, and when Fritz appeared, clad in his odd costume, he was greeted with applause. He seated himself with great gravity, his brothers pushed him off down the sandy beach, and the cajack glided into the water with inconceivable rapidity. The surface of the bay was calm, and soon the Greenlander was dancing gaily over the waves; then, like a skillful actor, he began executing a series of evolutions. Sometimes he would shoot off far out of our sight; then suddenly he would disappear in a cloud of foam, to the great terror of his mother; in another moment we saw his head above the floods, and an oar upraised to show his triumph.

At last he turned his frail bark towards Jackal River, and attempted to mount the current, but this proved too strong for him, and threw him back so violently that he disappeared from our sight. To jump into the canoe and fly to his assistance was the work of a moment. Jack and Ernest went with me, and we were growing uneasy when, suddenly, in the direction of a rock just visible through the foam, I saw a light cloud of smoke, which was shortly followed by a report.

I fired my pistol, which was instantly answered by another report in the same direction. After a hard row we perceived Fritz, and in a quarter of an hour we reached him.

We found him on the rocks. Before him lay a a walrus, or sea-cow, which he had killed with his harpoon. He explained how he had harpooned it twice, and at length shot it, and ended by saying gleefully that its fine head, with two great tusks, would make a capital ornament for the bow of his canoe. I felt that he had run some risk, as the animal turns when attacked, and was glad the adventure had ended so happily.

When he had finished cutting off its head, I wished to take him and his cajack into our canoe, but he refused, and dashed on, saying he would announce our return to his mother.

We arrived home safely, but only just in time, for a terrific storm came on, the flood-gates of heaven opened, and it was some time before we could venture out from the cave to see the damage.

The rain had been so abundant that Jackal River had overflowed its banks and damaged our bridge, which demanded instant restoration.

While we were occupied in considering these ravages chance caused us to make a new discovery; this was some small pears, about the size of plums, with which the sand was strewn. They looked so nice that the boys hastened to taste them, but they had scarcely touched them with their teeth than they threw them down in disgust. I wished to know what kind of fruit it was, and, taking one up, I recognised it as being the fruit of the clove-tree, another addition to our stock of spices.

We now employed ourselves in building protections against any other storms that might arise. Among other things I had long contemplated the erection of a drawbridge, and now appeared the proper time for constructing it. To be sure, a drawbridge was not a little thing to undertake, but after all that we had already done, we could not stop at the idea of constructing a bridge.

I understood the turning-bridges, but as I had neither vice nor windlass, I was obliged to adopt the simplest kind of drawbridge. I built between two high stakes a sweep that could be easily moved, and by the means of two ropes, a lever, and a counterpoise, we had a bridge which could be easily raised and lowered. It would only insure us against the invasion of animals, the river being too shallow to oppose any obstacle to a more serious attack. Such as it was, for a few days the new bridge was a great source of amusement to all the boys.

But, like all new inventions, the interest of the drawbridge quickly evaporated, and at the end of several days, if anyone climbed the stakes, it was that they might have the pleasure of seeing the antelopes and gazelles bounding over the plain near Falcon's Nest.

CHAPTER XXVIII

I RECEIVE A LETTER

As we had not been on an excursion for some time, I suggested that the boys should make one now, and in preparation for it I made them some pemmican, or pounded and crushed meat, which could be easily carried. For this purpose I used what remained of the bears' flesh, and, though they laughed at the idea of it at first, they were glad enough to take it, as it only occupied a small space in their bags.

The morning of departure arrived. Everyone was awake before day, and Jack, without saying a word to anybody, climbed up into the dove-cot, and took out several pairs of pigeons.

'How is this?' said I, as I saw the youngster placing his pigeons into a basket. 'They will be pretty tough eating.'

He looked at me knowingly for a moment, but did not answer.

Ernest alone remained with his mother and me, and we employed ourselves in constructing a sugar-cane press, of which my wife had much need.

The boys, meantime, had galloped off and passed over the tract of land that separated Family Bridge from another farm-colony not far from Prospect Hill, which we called the Hermitage, where they intended to pass the day, when, on approaching the farmhouse, they heard cries like that of a person in distress. It was a sort of wild, maniacal laugh, and the animals stopped in terror; the dogs barked and howled fearfully; and the ostrich, more frightened than the others, fled in the direction of the Lake of Swans with such rapidity that all the efforts of its master could not check it. The bull and the ass trembled so violently that Fritz and his brother were obliged to dismount.

Francis seized his gun, put two pistols in his belt, called the two dogs, and calmly walked on in the direction of the strange laugh. He had not gone more than thirty paces when he saw, through the bushes, an enormous hyena, which had killed one of our sheep, and was devouring it, while ever and anon that strange laugh of joy would echo from its blood-stained lips.

Francis placed himself behind a tree, and taking good aim, he discharged both barrels of his gun and broke the fore legs of the hyena. The dogs then rushed on, their terror changed into rage. The most terrible combat followed between them and the furious monster.

Fritz, who had tied the ass and the bull to a tree, now ran up. He and Francis would have fired again, but the dogs were so close to the hyena that they were afraid of hitting them, so that they were obliged to wait. Turk took the hyena by the throat and Flora by the muzzle, and there they held him until he dropped down dead.

Jack soon returned. He had not been able to stop the ostrich until it had arrived at the middle of the rice-field. Then they all admired the striped beast that lay before them. They took some trouble in dragging it to the farmhouse, where they settled for the night.

The following day was given to skinning the animal and preparing the hide.

In the meantime, we, who had been sitting quietly talking at home saw one of the pigeons, evidently coming from a distance, wheel round and alight on the dove-cot. I should not have noticed it, but Ernest, who had sprung to his feet, only waited until it entered the dove-cot, when he pulled the trap shut, and mysteriously disappeared. We took no notice of what he was doing, until he came back with a folded piece of paper in his hand, this he presented to me, saying it had just come by the post. I opened it and read:

'DEAR FATHER AND MOTHER,

'We arrived safely at the Hermitage, and there found a hyena, which had devoured several of our sheep. Francis has the honour of having killed the monster, and he behaved very pluckily. We have passed the whole day in preparing the skin, which is very fine and will be very useful. The pemmican is the most detestable stuff I ever tasted.

' Good-bye; much love from us all.

'FRITZ.'

113

I saw now at once why Jack had taken the pigeons, trusting to their instinct to return home, and we were delighted at his happy thought.

After dinner a new pigeon was seen to enter the dove-cot. Ernest, who had not remained quiet one moment during the day, rushed to capture it, and handed us a second letter. It ran as follows:

'The night has been fine — the weather beautiful — excursion in cajack on lake capture of some black swans — several new animals — sudden flight of an aquatic beast, entirely unknown to us — tomorrow at Prospect Hill.

　　　'Be of good cheer.
　　　　　　Your sons,
　　　　　　　　'FRITZ, JACK, AND FRANCIS.'

'It is like a telegram,' said I, laughing. 'Our huntsmen would rather fire a gun than write a sentence; nevertheless, I am glad to know they are safe.'

However, our rejoicing did not last long, for the very next day another pigeon arrived, with a letter telling us that on the boys' arrival at Prospect Hill they had found that the palisade, which we had erected at the end of the defile to keep out intruders from the desert, had been broken down, the sugar canes trampled and crushed, and that there were large marks everywhere, like those made by the feet of elephants. I resolved to go myself instantly to join the lads, and, having saddled the young colt, now almost as good a mount as its parent, I set off the same morning, leaving Ernest and his mother to follow later. When I arrived I found that the message had given me but a faint idea of the reality. The sugar canes were irretrievably lost; they had been trampled down, and the leaves torn off, by some animal that I was sure must have been an elephant. All our trouble in erecting the palisade had been wasted; the stakes had been torn up, the trees near by deprived of their bark, the bamboos had been treated no better than the sugar-canes, and every young shrub I had planted had been trampled.

Ernest and his mother arrived several hours after, bringing with them the waggon, drawn by the buffalo, the cow, and all necessary utensils for our encampment, which was likely to last a good while.

We immediately began the construction of a solid fortification across the defile, one that would effectually keep out all intruders. And this tiresome work occupied us constantly for more than a month.

When at last it was complete, our next labour was to build some sort of a fort to shelter us whenever we might visit the defile.

We chose four trees to answer the purpose, and did not cut the branches off close, but left them as rests for the beams of our platform.

We surrounded this platform when made with a high and strong network of rushes and branches, leaving an opening for entrance; and we covered the roof with the waterproof leaves of the Talipot palm. These leaves grow so large that ten men can be covered by one of them. Our fort was really rather like Falcon's Nest.

To ascend the platform, we cut notches in a beam which descended perpendicularly to the ground, and which could be raised and lowered at pleasure.

We did not, however, keep steadily to this work, but went off on various small expeditions in the meantime, and among our most important discoveries were some ripe bananas, and some of the great pods of the cocoa tree from which I promised I would make cocoa.

Fritz was the most adventurous, for he went off in his cajack the whole of one day, and following the coast line, penetrated further than any of us had ever done yet. He even went inland up the mouth of a great river he had found. He brought back a marvellous account of what he had seen, such as majestic forests, in which lived turkeys and peacocks, whose cries and screams imparted an air of life to the sombre river. Farther on, the scene had changed. There were enormous elephants feeding along the banks, in troops of twenty or thirty. Some were playing in the water, and squirting the cooling fluid over the heated bodies of their companions. Tigers and panthers, too, lay sleeping in the sun, their magnificent fur contrasting strangely with the green bank upon which they reclined; but not one of these animals paid the least attention to him.

What had frightened him most had been the sight of some great crocodiles, which had quickly made him retreat.

Even with the protection of the new palisade, I felt that this side of the island, near to all these dangerous beasts, was not so safe as the other, so I suggested we had been away from our fixed camp long enough, and should return to Falcon's Nest. This we did without any mishap.

It was some time after this — but indeed, time flowed so smoothly by, I forget exactly when — that Fritz, ever active, proposed we should make a fort on Shark Island, to which we could retire, if ever hard pressed by savage animals on land. I gave my assent, and we took there the two cannon we had brought from the ship. One can easily conceive how great were the obstacles that a man and four boys had to contend with, in order to convey two cannons to the island, and raise

115

them on a platform more than fifty feet in height. It cost us immense labour even to effect the transport of the cannons. This work took us a whole day of hard labour; but at last they were landed on a platform, and established with their mouths towards the sea. We placed a long pole in the rock, with a string and pulley, so that we could hoist up a flag at any time. How glad we felt when our work was done; and how proud we were of our ingenuity! When we had crowned this military construction with a flag, even though I felt we must be economical in our use of powder, we fired our cannons six times, and the echo of the rocks repeated the noise over the ocean.

CHAPTER XXIX

THE SHIPWRECKED SAILOR ON THE SMOKING ROCK

AS I have said, time glided away so fast, our days were filled with such varied labours and resources, that the wet seasons came and went with inconceivable rapidity, and I was startled to find, on reckoning up one day, that we had been ten years on our island.

The ten years were years of conquest and establishment. We had constructed several homes, built a solid wall across the defile, which would secure us against invasion from the wild beasts which infested the desert. The part of the country in which we lived was defended by high mountains on one side, and the ocean on the other; we had traversed the whole extent, and rested in perfect surety that no enemy lurked within it.

Cliff House was a safe retreat for us during the storms of winter, while Falcon's Nest was our summer residence and country villa; Prospect Hill and even our buildings at the Hermitage, were like the quiet farmhouses that the traveller finds in the mountains.

Of all our resources, the bees had prospered most; experience had taught me how to manage them, and the only trouble that I had was to provide new hives each year for the increasing swarms; and, in truth, so great was the number of our hives that they attracted a considerable flock of those birds called bee-eaters, who are extremely fond of these insects.

Our dove-cot had also succeeded well; and we had suspended baskets on the adjoining trees, where our pigeons might build their nests.

We also finished the gallery which extended along the front of our grotto; a roof was made to the rock above it, and it rested on fourteen columns of light bamboo, which gave it an elegant appearance; large pillars supported the gallery, around which twined the aromatic vines of the vanilla and the pepper, and each end of the gallery was terminated by a little cabinet with an elevated roof, having the appearance of a Chinese pavilion, surrounded by flowers and foliage. Steps led up into the gallery, which we had paved with a sort of stone so soft when dug out as to be cut easily with a chisel, but hardening rapidly in the sun.

The grounds of our home were pleasant; our plantations had succeeded, and between the grotto and the bay was a grove of trees and shrubs.

Shark Island no longer was an arid bank of sand: palm and pineapple trees had been planted everywhere, and the earth was covered with a carpet of vivid green. The scene around us was always animated and gay; the swans mingled with geese white as the driven snow, and the heron royal with his silvery crest, or the flamingo in his robe of rose colour, would stand by the marsh and capture the frogs with which it abounded. Under the shade of the beautiful trees our little troop of ostriches reposed, unmindful of the clamour raised by the flocks of cranes and turkeys that clustered around them; the Canada fowls and the heath-fowls, joining together and disdaining the society of their fellows, crossed to the other side of Family Bridge.

One could not recognise in this beautiful spot, surrounded by so much that was grateful to the eye and ear, the desert, sandy plain we had found on our first coming. It had for boundaries, on the right, Jackal River, which was bordered on our side by a strong and impenetrable hedge of thornpalms, aloes, Indian figs, karatas, and other plants of the same sort, all so close together that a mouse could scarcely penetrate it; on the left inaccessible rocks, among which was the grotto of crystal. Before us, as I have said, extended the blue sea, losing itself in the distance. Behind us the mass of rocks, in which our grotto was situated, was so high and steep that I feared nothing from that side.

The only outlet from our little elysium was Family Bridge, for which we had made a drawbridge; and that it might better be defended, we built a parapet of stones before it, and mounted on that two small six-pounder cannons, which could sweep the whole bay, while two others armed our ship of war, the celebrated pinnace.

A palisade of bamboos surrounded our garden, and added to the number of our defences. All our plantations were irrigated by tunnels of bamboo, which conveyed their supply of water from the river, and distributed it over the ground.

117

Our European trees had grown with a strength and rapidity of vegetation almost incredible; but their fruits had lost their flavour; and perhaps because the soil or the air was unfavourable, the apples and pears became black and withered, the plums and apricots were nothing but hard kernels surrounded by a tough skin; on the other hand, the indigenous productions multiplied a hundredfold: the bananas, the figs, the guavas, the oranges and the citron, made our corner of the island a paradise.

Our beautiful flowers also attracted numerous guests: these were the humming-birds; and it was one of our greatest amusements to watch these little birds flying around us, sparkling like precious stones, and hardly perceptible, so quick were their movements. They were passionate, choleric little fellows, and would attack others twice their size, and drive them away from their nests, and at other times they would tear in pieces the unlucky flower that had deceived their expectations of a feast.

The family of Turk and Flora had each year been increased by a certain number of puppies, out of which we had kept the healthiest, so that each member of the family now called a particular dog his own.

But the greatest changes of all were in my sons. When I thought of what children they were when I landed, I looked at them with thankfulness. Fritz had become a strong and vigorous man; although not tall, yet he was well proportioned. He was twenty-six years of age.

Ernest was twenty-four. He was not as strong as his brother, and his long limbs were rather too soft and rounded; he had a dreamy, meditative face.

Jack was lithe, light and supple, almost as much of a boy at twenty-three as he had been at thirteen; his whereabouts could always be known by his merry laugh.

Francis was sixteen. He promised to be even taller than Ernest, and was decidedly the best-looking of the four, with his clear, sun-tanned skin and fair hair. He was not so merry as Jack, so clever as Ernest, nor so capable as Fritz; but he was the best all-round man amongst them, and was distinguished for his good temper.

They had all grown up well-disposed, straight-forward, manly fellows, clean-hearted and fearless, and we had every reason to be proud of them.

Of course, now that my sons were men, I did not attempt to control them as I had formerly done, but let them go as they pleased on their own expeditions. Sometimes they were away for days together in different parts of the island.

On one occasion Fritz took with him some provisions, and went to sea in his cajack. He had set out before daylight, and when night was approaching nothing could be seen of him. My wife was in a state of the greatest suspense; and, to comfort her, I launched the canoe, and we set out for Shark Island. There, from the top of the flagstaff, we displayed our flag and fired a cannon. A few moments after we saw a black spot in the far distance, and, by the aid of a telescope, we discovered Fritz. He advanced slowly towards us, beating the sea with his oars, as if his canoe were charged with a double load.

As he came nearer we saw that his boat was filled with different things; and something heavy and dark, which looked like the head of a large animal, was being towed behind. He did not land, so we joined him on the water, and kept him company to the shore. But it was not until we had all arrived safely at Cliff House, that he told us anything. He explained he had gone for a considerable distance along the coast, and seen several walruses, and penetrated into a vast cave in which many little birds like swallows were flying about. He thought they were of the kind whose nests are eaten by the Chinese, being made of a sort of gummy moss, so he had procured some, and brought them back with him.

He had then gone on further until he had come to a great bay.

'While I was coasting along the shores of the bay,' he said, 'I saw at the bottom of the transparent waters, beds of shells resembling large oysters. I detached some with my hook, and threw them on the sand without getting out of my canoe, and set to work to obtain more. When I returned with a new load, I found that the oysters I had first deposited on the sand were opened, and the sun had already begun to corrupt them. I took up one or two; but instead of finding the nice fat oyster I expected, I found nothing but some gritty meat. In trying to detach this from the shell, I felt some little, round, hard stones, like peas, under my knife. I took them out, and found them so brilliant that I filled my pocket with them. Don't you think that they are really pearls?'

'See!' said his brothers, taking them in their hands. 'How beautiful, how brilliant, how regular!'

'They are really pearls,' cried I, 'oriental pearls of the greatest beauty. You have discovered a treasure, which one day will be, I hope, of immense value to us. We will pay a visit to this rich bag as soon as possible.'

Fritz did not appear much excited; jewels and money did not seem to him to be so valuable as he would once have thought them. He continued his story:

119

'As I was leaving the bay I saw on all sides, popping up out of the water, the heads of marine animals, which appeared about the size of a calf, and they plunged and frisked about in such a manner that I was afraid they would upset my cajack. So I secured it to a projecting rock, and, taking my eagle in my hand, I stood ready to attack the first that came near me. I then cast off my eagle, who soon seized on the largest and best, and blinded him. I jumped on the rock, and, catching hold of the animal with my boat-hook, drew it to the shore. All the others fled. Numbers of sea-birds clustered around me; gulls, sea-swallows, frigates, and half a dozen other kinds. They came up so close that I whirled my staff around to keep them off, and in doing so knocked down a very large bird, an albatross, I think. I fastened my sea-otter to the stern of my boat, and, taking a sackful of oysters, returned home again.'

When he had finished, after talking a little of what he had told us, the others dispersed, and Fritz took the opportunity to tell me about something still more strange that he had discovered.

'In examining the albatross which I had knocked down,' he said, 'I saw a piece of linen around one of its feet. I untied it, and read the following words written upon it in good English: "*Save the poor ship-wrecked sailor on the smoking rock.*" The bird was only stunned so I wrote on a strip of my handkerchief: "*Have faith in God: help is near.*" And if by any chance the bird goes back to the place it came from, it may do good.'

I was, of course, much interested in this curious fact, but knowing that the albatross travels immense distances, I thought it hardly likely that the man who sent the message was anywhere near us, especially as the message itself might be years old.

After this we examined the sea-otter that Fritz had brought back, and once again discussed the subject of the pearls. The others were naturally anxious to go and fish for some more themselves, and this we decided to do.

Accordingly, we gathered together all the implements we thought likely to be of use in this strange new fishery and prepared our provisions for the voyage: two hams were cooked, cassava cakes barley-bread, rice, nuts, almonds, and dry fruits; and for drink we took a barrel of water, and one of honey-syrup. These stores, with our tools and fishing implements, loaded down the boat.

The next day a fresh and favourable breeze and a slightly ruffled sea induced us to embark immediately. Francis and his mother were left at home, and we gaily put off, amid their prayers and wishes for our safe return. We took with us young Nip, the successor of our good old monkey, and two of our dogs. Jack occupied a second seat in Fritz's cajack. Ernest and I conducted the canoe loaded with our provisions and animals.

The cajack led the way and we followed, steering our course through the shoals and rocks with the greatest difficulty. We did not encounter any marine monsters; but the rocks were covered with the whitened bones of walruses and sea-horses, and Ernest made us stop several times, at the risk of bruising our boat against the rocks, in order that he might collect some of these remains for our museum of natural history.

The sea was as calm and brilliant as a mirror, and was covered with the little boats of the nautilus, a sort of shell-fish which much resembles a miniature gondola.

My sons could not behold these beautiful little boats, dancing over the surface of the waves, without wishing to capture some; they threw out a net, and we caught half a dozen fine ones.

We soon attained the promontory behind which, Fritz said, was the Bay of Pearls. This promontory was singular and imposing. Arch rose above arch, column above column; in a word, it resembled the front of one of those old Gothic cathedrals, covered with a thousand carvings. The only difference was that, instead of a pavement of marble, we had the blue sea, and the columns were washed by the waves. We rowed into the great cavern and sent the startled birds flying in all directions.

When our eyes became habituated to the darkness, we saw that every niche and comer was filled with their nests. These nests resembled white cups, were as transparent as horn, and filled, like the nests of other birds, with feathers, and dry sticks of some sort of perfumed wood.

I resolved to gather a considerable number of them, only taking care to leave those which contained eggs or young ones. Fritz and Jack climbed like cats along the rocks and detached the nests, which they gave to Ernest and me, who placed them in a large sack we had brought. Afterwards I set Ernest to work to clear the nests of the feathers and dirt.

When this was done, we passed on to the beautiful bay Fritz had christened the Bay of Pearls. The water was so calm and pure that we could see the fish far below us. I recognised a sort of white fish, the shining scales of which are used as false pearls. I showed them to my sons; but they could not understand how a little stone would be worth so much more than the fish-scales, when the latter were quite as brilliant.

At last we arrived at the rocky bank where Fritz had found the pearl oysters. The coast presented a most beautiful prospect; forests, which lost themselves in the distance, and high mountains covered with the rich vegetation of the tropics. A majestic river flowed into the bay, and cut the green prairies like a band of silver. We all landed safely except the monkey, who could not make up his mind to leap the narrow space which separated him from the land. Twenty times he rose on his hind legs, and twenty times he shrank back, as if he had the ocean to cross. At length we took pity on him, and threw him a rope, by which means he landed safely.

The day was too far advanced to begin our pearlfishing, so we had our dinner consisting of some slices of ham, fried potatoes, and cassava cakes; and, after having lighted fires along the coast, to keep off wild beasts, we left the dogs on shore, and went on board the canoe. We drew the sail over our heads, and, wrapping ourselves in our bear skins, were soon asleep. Nothing disturbed us save a concert of jackals.

We rose at daylight, and after breakfast began our labours in the pearl-fishery, and with the aid of the rakes, hooks, nets, and poles, soon brought in a large quantity of the precious oysters. We heaped them all up in a pile on the shore, so that the heat of the sun would cause them to open.

Towards evening the coast appeared so beautiful, and the vegetation so rich and glowing, that it was impossible for us to resist the temptation of making an excursion to a little wood, where we had heard turkeys gobbling all day. Each took his own way.

But my discovery was the most important. Seeing Nip gathering some large black tubercles, with which the ground was covered, I picked up two or three which I put in my game-bag; and when I examined them later, found they were truffles, of a perfumed, delicate flesh, marbled with white.

Here was another luxury which many a gourmand in Europe would have been delighted with. When night came we lighted our watch fires, had our dinner, and then retired to our canoe. The dogs were again left on shore.

CHAPTER XXX

ATTACKED BY LIONS

THE next day Ernest and Jack, having been off again, returned from the woods together, with a fine boar which they had shot, and having heard that boar's head was good eating, we resolved to cook it with truffles, in the Otaheitan manner. Consequently Fritz and Ernest set to work, and dug a deep ditch, while I cleaned the head and heated some stones. When these preparations were finished, we placed the head, stuffed with truffles, and seasoned with salt, pepper, and nutmeg, in the ditch, and covered it with red-hot stones and a thick layer of earth. While our supper was cooking, we suspended the hams of the boar over the smoke of the fire, and sat down to talk over the events of the day, when, suddenly, a deep prolonged roar rang through the forest. It was the first time we had ever heard such unearthly tones. The rocks echoed it, and we felt seized with sudden terror. The dogs and the jackals also started howling horribly.

'What a diabolical concert!' said Fritz, jumping up and seizing his gun. 'Build up the fire, and while I try to discover the danger in my cajack, you retreat to the boat.'

This plan appeared the best we could pursue, and I adopted it. We threw on the fire all the wood we could find ready cut, and, without losing time, we reached the boat; but it was tethered to a great stone, and whether our hands were trembling, or from whatever other cause, we fumbled at the rope without undoing it. Fritz jumped into the cajack, and was soon lost in the darkness of the night, which was now closing in.

During all this time the roarings continued, and they appeared to approach nearer to us. Our dogs gathered around the fire, uttering plaintive moans. Our poor little monkey seemed to be terrified. I imagined that the wild beast which made this hideous din must be a leopard or a panther, which had been attracted by the remains of the wild boar in the wood. My doubts did not last long, for we soon discovered by the light of our fires, a terrible lion, considerably larger and stronger than those I had seen in the menageries of Europe. In two or three leaps he bounded over the space which separated the wood from the shore. He stood immovable for a moment, and then, lashing his flanks with his tail, and roaring furiously, crouched down as if to spring on us. Meantime I felt wildly in my pockets for a knife, but could find none. I could not understand why my sons did not fire, but discovered afterwards that they, like myself, had left their guns on shore. The frightful pantomime did not last long. The lion's flaming eyes were fixed directly on us. Suddenly I heard a report. The animal bounded up, gave a tremendous yell, and fell lifeless on the earth.

'Tis Fritz,' murmured Ernest, pale with terror.

'Yes,' I cried, 'Fritz has saved us!'

We all sprang on shore, but our dogs, with an admirable instinct, began to bark again. I did not neglect this indication. We threw more wood on the fire, and again jumped into the boat. It was time; for scarcely were we there, and had managed to cast off, when a second enemy rushed from the forest. It was not so large as the first, but its roar was frightful. It was a lioness. She was seeking her mate, and running straight up to his body, she smelled it, and licked it; and when she found that he was dead she set up a howl of rage, lashed her sides, and opened her mouth, as if she would devour us all.

Again Fritz fired, and the shot, less fortunate than the first, only broke the shoulder of the animal. The wounded lioness rolled on the sand, foaming with rage, but all three of our dogs rushed upon her. I jumped from the boat, and, running up to the animal who was held fast by the dogs, I plunged my hunting-knife right into her heart, and she rolled over dead in an instant. But the victory had cost us dear, for there lay one of our dogs, a second Flora, dying from the terrible wounds she had received.

Fritz ran up, so did Ernest and Jack, and lighting some torches, we gazed at the lions majestically extended on the sand.

'What a terrible range of teeth!' said Ernest, as he raised up the head of the lion.

'Yes, and what frightful claws!' said Jack. 'Wouldn't they make nice holes in your skin?'

'Poor Flora!' said Fritz, as he detached the dead body of our dog from that of the lioness; 'she has done for us to-day what our old ass did in the case of the boa. Come, Ernest, see if you cannot make an epitaph.'

'I am not in the mood to make rhymes,' said Ernest, who still looked much upset.

Flora the second received the honours of a funeral by torchlight. We dug a grave, and silently placed in it the remains of the devoted animal, with a flat stone to mark her resting-place. Ernest wrote above it:

124

HERE LIES

FLORA, A DOG

REMARKABLE FOR HER COURAGE AND DEVOTION.

SHE DIED UNDER THE CLAWS OF A LION

ON WHOM SHE ALSO INFLICTED DEATH

'It is only prose,' he said, 'but it must do.'

Jack, who did not care much for poetry or prose, remarked that we had better have something to eat.

'I suppose,' said he, 'the boar's head must be done by this time; anyway, I mean to go and see.'

So saying he began to clear away the covering of earth and cinders, while Ernest and I dressed the wounds of the other dogs. But instead of the juicy meat poor Jack expected, he found nothing but a mass of bones and burned flesh. He was going to throw it away in disgust, when I stopped him, and, cutting off the burned part with my knife, we found underneath some most delicious meat, saturated with the perfume of the truffles in a manner that every epicure knows how to appreciate.

When we had eaten, we tried to snatch a little sleep, but were too excited to do more than doze fitfully. At sunrise we were up, and our first care was to take off the lions' skins. My syringe, which I had brought with me, did the business effectually, and we soon obtained two of the most splendid skins that can be imagined. The fur was as soft as silk, and of a most beautiful colour.

The heat of the sun had begun to corrupt the oysters heaped upon the bank, and the effluvia which they exhaled induced us to return to Cliff House, for we meant to come back to get the pearls when the sun and air had sufficiently dried the oysters to make the task endurable.

Early next morning we set sail. Jack did not feel much inclination to take his place again in Fritz's cajack, so embarked with us in the boat.

Fritz set off before us, as if to serve as pilot; but when he had conducted us through the vault and over the shoals, he rowed up to our boat, and, handing me a letter, shot off again like an arrow. I opened the paper quickly, and imagine my surprise when I found that, instead of having forgotten the albatross and the smoking rock, he informed me in the letter that he was going in search of the unfortunate being. I had a thousand objections to make to this project, but Fritz rowed so fast I could barely halloo through the speaking-trumpet, 'Return soon, and be prudent,' before he was out of sight. We gave to the cape where he left us the name of the 'Adieu Cape.'

We arrived at Cliff House without accident, and the different treasures we had brought were joyfully received; the truffles, the lionskins, the pearls, the birds'-nests, became the objects of a thousand questions, but they could not drive away the thoughts of Fritz, and my wife said she would willingly give up all our cargo if she could be sure of his safety.

I had not yet spoken to her concerning the reason of Fritz's absence, as I had not wished to give rise to hopes which were so unlikely to be realised; but now I thought I might, so I told her of his quest.

Then we began the preparation of our lion-skins, and carried them for that purpose to our tannery on Whale Island, where, as I said before, our dirty work was done. We also occupied ourselves in storing our provisions, and with the necessary household duties.

Five days passed away, and still Fritz had not returned, and his mother was so anxious and worried that I proposed to launch the pinnace and make a new excursion to the Bay of Pearls. This time we took her and Francis with us, and she received my proposition to that effect with pleasure, for she thought that Fritz would return in that direction, and that we should certainly meet him. We lost no time; the pinnace was prepared, and early the next day we set out, and were in sight of the promontory of the bay, when suddenly the vessel ran against a black mass, and was nearly thrown over by the shock. My wife uttered a cry, but the boat soon righted, and I perceived that the obstacle was not a rock, as I had thought, but a whale. I instantly pointed the cannons of the pinnace, and a discharge of artillery prevented him from overturning us, which he certainly would have done if the blow had not stunned him. We saw with pleasure that the waves carried the enormous body to a sandbank a little distance from the shore, and there it lay like a stranded ship.

While we were talking about it, Ernest suddenly uttered a loud cry.

'A man! a savage!' said he; and he pointed out to us in the distance a sort of canoe dancing over the waves. The occupant seemed to have perceived us, for he advanced, and then disappeared behind a projecting point, as if to communicate his discovery to his companions. I had not the slightest doubt that we had fallen in with a band of savages,

126

and we began to fortify our boat against their arrows by making a bulwark of the stalks of maize and corn we had brought with us. We loaded our cannons, guns, and pistols; and, everything arranged, we stood ready behind our rampart, resolved to defend it as long as we were able. We dared not advance, for there was the savage; until Ernest, growing tired of the pantomime, observed that, if we used the speaking-trumpet, possibly our savage might understand some words of the half-dozen languages we were familiar with.

The advice appeared good. I took up the speaking-trumpet and bellowed out with all my force some words of Malay; but still the canoe remained immovable, as if its master had not comprehended us.

'Instead of Malay,' said Jack, 'suppose we try English.'

So saying, he caught up the trumpet, and in his clear, loud tone pronounced some common sailor phrases, well known to all who have ever been on board ship. The device succeeded, and we saw the savage advancing toward us, holding a green branch in his hand. Nearer and nearer he came, and at last we recognised in the painted savage our own dear Fritz.

'Fritz! 'Tis Fritz — 'tis Fritz! There is his cajack and the walrus's head in front. It is Fritz disguised like a savage,' exclaimed Jack.

We soon received him in astonishment. He was naked to the waist, and painted white and black, just like a Carribee Indian.

CHAPTER XXXI

A VISITOR

WE all laughed and talked together so much at first we could hardly understand why he had behaved in this way; but the first words I caught clearly were: 'My quest has been successful.' This he said in a low voice to me.

'As for my costume,' he continued aloud, 'as I have been a considerable distance, I disguised myself by painting the upper part of my body with powder, soaked in water, in case I fell in with savages, who would have killed a white man at sight. When I saw you and knew you did not recognise me, I could not resist teasing you a little.'

We all began to laugh over the farce; and Fritz, drawing me aside, said, in an eager, joyous tone:

'I have succeeded, I have found a poor shipwrecked girl — for it was a woman that had written those lines. Three years has she lived on that smoking rock, all alone destitute of everything! Can you believe it? But the poor girl has begged me not to betray her sex, except to you and my mother, for she is dressed as a man, and is shy and nervous, although I assured her that all of us would welcome her gladly. I have brought her with me; she is near by, on a little island just beyond the Bay of Pearls; come and see her, but do not say anything to the others; I want to give them a surprise.'

I agreed, and ordered them to hoist the sails, weigh anchor, and make ready to depart. Fritz, who had changed his dress and washed off his disguise, flew about, hastening his less eager brothers; then, jumping into his cajack, he piloted us through the shoals and reefs that were scattered along the coast. After an hour's sailing he turned off, and directed his course towards a shady island not far from the Bay of Pearls; we sailed close up to the shore, and fastened the pinnace to the trunk of a fallen tree. Fritz, however, was quicker than we, and he was on shore, and had entered a little wood in the middle of the island before we had yet landed. We followed him into the wood, and soon found ourselves near a hut, built like those of the Hottentots, with a fire burning before it, on which some fish were being cooked in a large shell. Fritz uttered a halloo, and what was our surprise to see, descending from a large tree, a young and handsome sailor, who, turning his timid eyes on us, stood still, as if he dared not approach!

It was such a long time since we had seen a man — ten years! —society had become so strange a thing to us, that we remained stupefied.

The silence was broken by Fritz, who, taking the young sailor by the hand, advanced toward us.

'Father, mother!' said he, in a voice brimming over with excitement, 'here is a friend — a brother, a new companion in misfortune — Sir Edward Montrose, who, like ourselves, has been shipwrecked on the coast.'

'He is welcome among us,' was the general cry; and, approaching the young sailor, whom I easily recognised for a woman, I took her by the hand and comforted and encouraged her.

Once the ice was broken, all joined in a hearty greeting, and question after question poured upon Fritz, who joyfully replied:

'I will tell you all afterwards; let us attend now to our new brother.'

Supper was served, and my wife brought out a bottle of her spiced hydromel to add to the feast.

128

Everybody spoke at once, and my sons addressed their new companion with such vivacity as to embarrass the timid stranger; my wife saw his distress, and, as it was late, she gave the signal for a general break-up, saying she was going to make up a bed for our visitor on the pinnace, where he could sleep comfortably. My sons and I stopped to light and arrange our watch-fires.

The new-comer naturally became the subject of conversation.

'I should like to know,' said Francis, addressing himself to Fritz, 'where you found this man?'

Fritz smiled without answering.

But after a few minutes he recounted to his brothers the whole history of the albatross; as he spoke of his thoughts and actions, he became so excited in his narration, that he forgot himself and the secret that he had to keep, and he called the young sailor 'Emily.'

'Emily! — Emily!' repeated his brothers, who had begun to doubt the mystery, 'Emily! — Fritz has deceived us, and Sir Edward is a girl! — our adopted brother turned into a sister!'

This discovery changed the conversation. Fritz explained to his brothers that Emily, appearing in a midshipman's dress, which she had habitually worn while alone, had been ashamed at first to say she was a girl; but the boys declared that nothing pleased them better than to have a new sister, and that this change would not lower Emily at all in their esteem.

The next morning it was a a comic sight to see the embarrassment and awkwardness with which they approached one whom they had the day before greeted as a comrade. As for Emily, she was very much astonished at the discovery the young men had made, and she retreated to my wife; but a moment after, recovering herself, she advanced, and extending her hand to each of the boys, gracefully demanded for the sister the friendship they had extended to the brother. This amiable frankness dissipated the embarrassment of my three sons; they assured the young girl of their fraternal regard, and begged that they might consider her as a sister. Gaiety was re-established, and we sat down to breakfast, which was composed of fruits, cold meat, and chocolate of our own making — a great treat to my new daughter. Shortly after breakfast she retired with my wife, who lent her some of her own garments, so that she need no longer feel the embarrassment of her clothes.

Then I proposed we should go back to the island to get what we should find useful from the stranded whale.

After staying a day or two longer here in order to undertake this disagreeable task, we thought of returning to Cliff House. We packed up everything we had, including Emily's treasures, both those she had saved from shipwreck and those she had made herself. Fritz had given her a box which held them all, and they really were very curious, consisting of clothes, ornaments, domestic utensils, and all sorts of articles which she had made in her exile, out of the scanty material she had at her disposal. There were fish-lines of the twisted hair of her head, with fish-hooks attached, made of mother-of-pearl; some needles fashioned from fish-bones; piercers and bodkins, which had once been the beaks of birds; two beautiful needle-cases, one made of a pelican's feather, the other of the bone of a sea-calf. The skin of a young walrus sewed together served for a bottle; a lamp made of a shell, with a wick of cotton drawn from her hand-kerchief; over the lamp another shell served as boiler; a turtle-shell used for cooking food, by the throwing in of hot stones; some fish-bladders, shells of all sizes, serving for glasses, spoons, dishes, etc.; little sacks full of seeds, a quantity of plants, such as the cochelaria, sorrel, celery, and cress, which grow among the rocks.

For clothing she had a hat made of the downy breast of the cormorant, which was stretched over some feathers from the same bird, forming a complete shelter for the head and neck against the rays of the sun, a little waistcoat with sleeves, made from the skin of the sea-calf, the skin of the fore legs serving as sleeves; some other garments of bird-skin or walrus-skin; and belts, stockings, and shoes all of skin; besides the midshipman's uniforms which she had found in a stranded chest.

Emily's jewels were few in number, consisting of a gold comb and a string of fine pearls, which she happened to have on when shipwrecked; she had also some boxes made of turtle-shells, which contained pieces of amber, and some pearls of a beautiful red tint, which she had extracted from some sort of shell-fish, and besides, some pencils made of feathers and hair, with which she had amused herself by writing. I must not forget to mention a beautiful little purse made of sea-calf-skin, and containing some rare shells which she had gathered on the seashore.

The next day, when we were all ready to start. Emily brought us another proof of her patience and industry; she ran into a little plot of shrubbery, the branches of which dipped into the sea, and brought out a large bird, tied by a cord, which she presented to us, telling us it was a skilful fisherman — a cormorant — which she had trained and taught, after the manner of the Chinese, to capture fish.

We then left the bay which we named Happy Bay, and set off, intending to call at the Bay of Pearls on our way back.

Fritz, seated in his cajack, served as pilot to assist us in penetrating safely through the rocks and shoals, and we arrived there in safety. Everything was found just as we had left it — the table and benches yet standing, our fireplace undestroyed, and what was more, the air was purified, and the oysters, having all been dried up by the sun, had lost their unpleasant odour. The dead bodies of the lions and the wild boar were but heaps of whitened bones, the birds of prey having completely stripped them of every particle of flesh.

All appeared tranquil, and we thought it safe to stop long enough to extract the pearls from their shells; this operation, which was certainly not very agreeable, did not long detain Emily, who ran away.

She took her cormorant under her arm, and jumping into the cajack, in two strokes of the oars was twenty paces from the shore; she then passed a large copper ring round the neck of the cormorant, so that he could not swallow the fish he caught. Thus prepared, she placed him on the edge of the boat, and remained perfectly still.

The fishing soon commenced, and it was a droll sight to see the feathered fisherman, his neck stretched out, his eye fixed steadily on the water. Every now and then he gave a plunge and reappeared with a fine fish — a trout, a silver-fish or a salmon — which he carried to his young mistress. After he had caught enough, she took the ring off his neck, gave him some of the fish as a reward, and returned.

When our pearls were all extracted we counted them and found four hundred, among which were some extraordinarily large ones. There was nothing for supper except Emily's fish; my sons, therefore, took their guns and game-bags, intending to go and shoot some birds in the Wood of Truffles. Emily went with them, and having killed a snipe on the wing, elicited unbounded applause from my sons, who, when they returned home, lauded her performance to the skies.

CHAPTER XXXII

THE RETURN TO CLIFF HOUSE

ON our way to Cliff House I asked Emily to tell us her own story, and give us some account of her shipwreck. She was lively enough, and made no difficulty. She told us that she was born in India, of English parents, and that her father was a colonel, named Sir Edward Montrose. He lost his wife only three years after his marriage; and all his affections centred in their only child. He was lucky enough to obtain a command in an English colony, so that he need not be separated from her. He educated her himself, teaching her outdoor sports as well as book-work. At the age of eighteen, she managed a rifle as well as a needle, and was as much at home in the saddle as on her feet.

Colonel Montrose was then ordered to return with his regiment to England. This circumstance forced him to separate himself from his daughter who could not travel on a troop-ship. It was arranged, however, that she should sail the same day that he did, in another ship.

The voyage at first was prosperous and agreeable, but before many days a terrible storm arose. The ship was thrown off her course, and a furious wind drove her down upon our rocky coast; two boats were launched upon the angry waves. Emily found a place in the smallest — the captain was in the other. The storm continuing, the boats were soon separated, and the one that contained Emily broken in pieces, and she alone, of all the crew, was fortunate enough to escape death. The waves carried her, half-fainting, to the foot of the rock where Fritz discovered her. She crawled under the shade of a rock, and, sinking on the sand, slept for four-and-twenty hours. There she passed several days with no nourishment but some birds' eggs, which she found on the rocks. At the end of that time, the sun reappearing and the sea growing calm, she thought of the crew in the other boat, and in the hope that they might see her, she established signals of distress.

In wandering about the rocks she came upon much wreckage, which convinced her the ship had completely broken up. Among other things she found the midshipman's chest, and she accordingly dressed herself in the uniform of a midshipman, which she had worn ever since. Among other things were some matches, still unspoilt by damp, as the chest was closely fastened. So she picked up some pieces of wood which the sea had thrown on the sand, carried them to the summit of the rock, and there kindled a fire, which she never allowed to go out. Later, she built a hut, fished, hunted, tamed birds — among others the cormorant — and she lived alone for three long dreary years.

As Emily stopped I saw Fritz's eyes meet hers, which fell before them, and the dear girl blushed. Then arose in me a hope, which my wife afterwards assured me had been in her mind since the first moment she saw them together.

When we came in sight of Prospect Hill I proposed to stop and take a look at the farm house; but Fritz and Francis, who were in the cajack, said they would go straight on home, so that they could have everything prepared for us. All was in order at the farmhouse. Emily, who for three years had not seen a human habitation, could not restrain a cry of admiration. My wife showed her the colonies of fowls which she had established, and which had prospered beyond our hopes.

We again embarked in the pinnace, and from Prospect Hill we sailed to Shark Island, where we secured, in passing, a quantity of the soft wool of the Angora rabbit. From Shark Island we directed our course toward Cliff House, and could just distinguish it, when a salute greeted our ears.

We returned the polite salute, and soon after we saw Fritz and Francis coming toward us in their canoe. They received us at the entrance of the bay, and followed us to the shore. They landed before us, and the moment Emily's foot touched the sand a hurrah resounded through the air, and Fritz, springing forward, led her up to the grotto. There a surprise awaited us. A table was spread in the middle of the gallery, and loaded with all the fruits that the country produced. Bananas, figs, guavas, oranges, rose up in perfumed heaps upon flat calabashes. All the vases of our making, coconut cups and ostrich eggs mounted on turned wooden pedestals, urns of painted porcelain all were filled with hydromel and milk; while a large dish of fried fish, and a huge roast turkey, stuffed with truffles, formed the solid part of the repast. A double festoon of flowers surrounded the canope above the table, and on it was a large medallion, on which was inscribed, 'Welcome, fair Emily Montrose!' It was a complete holiday, and as grand a reception as our means would allow. Emily sat down to table between my wife and myself; Ernest and Jack also took their places; while the two caterers of the feast, each with a napkin on his arm, did the honours of the table. Toasts were drunk, and Emily's name echoed from every side.

We passed from the table to the grotto, and she was delighted with all she saw. We led her to the kitchen-garden; we showed her our orchard, our dove-cot — not a corner passed unnoticed. Falcon's Nest next received a visit; it had fallen into decay from neglect, and we passed a whole week in fitting it up. We then set out for the Hermitage, to gather our rice and other grains; for the season was advancing, and some violent showers already warned us to hasten our preparations for the coming winter. Emily gave proof, during these labours, of an intelligence and good-will which rendered her assistance very valuable; and she inspired everybody with such zeal and industry that when the win-

133

ter set in we were all prepared for it. Ten years had accustomed us to the terrible winters, and we calmly listened to the wind and storm as it raged furiously without. We had reserved for the winter several occupations, in which our new companion proved her skill and industry. She excelled in weaving and plaiting straw and osiers, and under her directions, we made some light straw hats for summer, some baskets, and conveniently arranged game-bags. My wife was delighted with her adopted daughter, and Ernest found a companion who could talk to him about literature and poetry. In fact, Emily had become to my wife and myself a fifth child, and to my sons a sister.

CHAPTER XXXIII

AN ENGLISH SHIP

IT was toward the end of the rainy season, the wind had lost its violence, and a patch of blue sky could now and then be seen; our pigeons had quitted the dove-cot, and we ourselves ventured to open the door of the grotto and taste the fresh air.

Our first care was for our gardens, which had suffered injury; we took account of the damage as well as we were able, and then set out for our more distant possessions. Fritz and Jack proposed to make an excursion to Shark Island, to inspect our fort and colony there. I consented, and they set off in the cajack.

When they arrived they examined the interior of the fort, and found that nothing of importance was damaged. Then, wishing to see whether the cannons were in good order, they fired one off. What was their astonishment when, a moment after, they heard distinctly three reports of cannon in the distance. They could not be mistaken, for a faint light toward the east preceded each report. After an excited conversation as to what should be done, they jumped into the canoe and made for home to tell us the news.

We had heard the report of the cannon they had fired, and we could not imagine why they were hurrying back so fast. As soon as they came within earshot I called out as loud as I could:

'Halloo, there! what is the matter?'

On they came, and jumping on shore, shouted out: 'Did you not hear them?'

'Hear what?' said I. 'We have heard nothing but the noise your waste of powder made.'

'You have not heard three other reports in the distance?'

'No.'

'Why, we heard them plainly and distinctly.'

'It was the echo,' said Ernest.

This remark nettled Jack a little, and he replied rather sharply:

'No, Mr. Doctor, it wasn't the echo; I think I have fired cannon enough in my lifetime to know whether that was an echo or not. We distinctly heard three reports of a cannon, and we are certain that some ship is sailing in this part of the world.'

'If there is really a ship on our coasts,' said I, 'who knows whether it is manned by Europeans or by pirates?'

Until we knew this we felt we should be on our guard, so we took turns at watching, but the night passed quietly away, and in the morning the rain began again, and continued so violently during two days that it was impossible for us to go out.

On the third day the sun reappeared. Fritz and Jack, full of impatience, resolved to return to Shark Island, and try a new signal. I consented; but instead of the cajack we took the canoe, and I went with them. The others stayed at home. On arriving at the fort we hoisted our flag, while Jack, ever impatient, loaded a cannon and fired it; but scarcely had the report died away in the distance, when we distinctly heard a louder answering report in the direction of Cape Disappointment or Prospect Bay.

Jack could not contain himself for joy.

'Men, men,' cried he, jumping in his excitement, 'are you sure of it now?'

And his enthusiasm communicating itself to us, we hoisted another and a larger flag on our flag staff. Six other reports followed the first one we had heard.

We felt it best to return to the shore, for from the direction of the sound, the ship was probably at anchor in Prospect Bay. The others had seen our flags flying, and bombarded us with questions.

'Quick, tell us,' cried they, all at once, 'are they Europeans? — English? — is it a merchant vessel? — a steamer?'

We could not answer; we could only positively say we were sure there was a ship of some kind. My sons were half wild with joy; and Emily especially, giving rein to her imagination, assured me that it was certainly her father come in search of her.

As the shots had come from the direction of the bay beyond Falcon's Nest, thither we all set out, Fritz and I in the cajack, the rest by land.

Fritz and I went along fast, and when we rounded the promontory we saw suddenly a fine ship at anchor, with a long-boat at the side, and an English flag floating at the masthead.

How can I describe what we felt? After all these years we were almost overcome at the idea of again facing strangers. Fritz would have thrown himself into sea and swum off to the ship; but I was afraid that, notwithstanding the English flag, the vessel before us might be a pirate, which had assumed false colours in order to deceive us. We remained at a distance, not liking to venture nearer until we were certain what ship it was. We could see all that was going on. Two tents had been raised on the shore, tables were laid for dinner, meat was roasting before blazing fires, men were running to and fro, and the whole scene had the appearance of an organised encampment. Two sentinels were on the deck of the vessel, and when they perceived us they spoke to the officer on duty who stood near, and who turned his telescope toward us.

'They are Europeans,' cried Fritz; 'you can easily judge from the face of the officer.'

Fritz's remark was true; but yet I did not like to go too near. We remained in the bay, manoeuvring our canoe, and I cried out through my speaking-trumpet these three words, *Englishmen, good men*! But no answer was returned; our cajack, and more than all, our home-made costumes, I expect, made them take us for savages. Then the officer made signs to us to approach, and held up knives, scissors, and glass beads. This mistake made us laugh; but we did not approach, as we wished to present ourselves before him better fitted out.

We hastened instead to land near Falcon's Nest, where the others had already arrived. Every one but myself and my wife was half mad with joy; they ran hither and thither, hardly knowing what they did. As for myself, I scarcely wished to renounce my life and my possessions, which had cost me so much labour, and had become so dear to me; and neither my wife nor myself could again consent to a sea voyage; but all this was merely a dream; we as yet knew nothing about the ship or its character.

We spent some time in preparing the pinnace, and loading it with presents for the captain. When we at last set off we sailed gallantly along, Fritz preceding us as pilot. Ernest, Jack, and Francis managed the boat, while I attended to the tiller. As a precaution we loaded our cannons and guns, and took with us all the defensive arms that we could find, in case of accidents.

When we drew near to the ship, a sensation of joy was experienced by us all: my sons were dumb with pleasure and eagerness.

'Hoist the English flag,' cried I, and a second after, a flag similar to the one on the ship fluttered from our masthead.

If we were filled with extraordinary emotions on seeing a European ship, the English were not less astonished to see a little boat with flowing sails coming toward them. Guns were now fired from the ship and answered from our pinnace, and joining Fritz in his cajack, we approached nearer.

The captain received us with that frankness and cordiality that always distinguish sailors; and I went down with him to the cabin, where wine was set out. He told us his name was Littelton.

I related to him as briefly as possible the history of our shipwreck, and of our residence of ten years on this coast. I spoke to him of Emily, and asked him if he had ever heard of Sir Edward Montrose. The captain not only knew him, but said that it was a part of his instructions to explore these latitudes, where, three years before, the ship *Dorcas* which had on board the daughter of Colonel Montrose, was supposed to be wrecked, and to try to discover whether anything concerning the vessel or crew could be ascertained. He told me that a storm lasting four days had thrown him off the course, which he followed for Sydney and New Holland; and thus he had been driven on this coast, where he had renewed his wood and water. 'It was then,' added he, 'that we heard the reports of cannon, which we answered; on the third day new discharges convinced us that were were not alone on the coast, and we resolved to wait until, by some means or other, we discovered who were our companions in misfortune. But we find an organised colony and a maritime power, whose alliance I solicit in the name of the sovereign of Great Britain.'

We then went on deck, where he spoke kindly to Emily, and told her that her father was alive and well.

The captain had brought with him an English family, consisting of Mr. Wolston, a distinguished engineer, who had come in search of health, his wife, and two daughters. They had all been much upset during the storm, and gladly accepted our invitation to spend the night with us at Cliff House. The captain would have been pleased to come too, but did not like to leave his ship.

137

It is difficult to express the astonishment which was evinced by the Wolston family on seeing all our arrangements. We showed them the giant tree of Falcon's Nest, and Cliff House, with its rocky vault. We all had supper together in the verandah at Cliff House, and then made up beds for our guests.

The next morning Mr. Wolston came up to me, and shaking my hand heartily, said, 'I cannot express all the admiration that I feel on seeing what you have done. The hand of God has been with you, and here you live happily, far away from the strife of the world, alone with your family. I came from England to seek rest: where can I find it better than here? I shall be the happiest of men if you will allow me to establish myself in a corner of your domains.'

I assured him that nothing would give me greater pleasure.

He told his wife of my assent, and she was as much pleased as he. But I was thinking of more difficult problems. The ship was only the second we had seen in ten years, and probably as long a period might elapse before another appeared, should we let Captain Littelton leave us, and not take advantage of this opportunity to return to a civilized country?

My wife did not wish to go. I was myself too much attached to my life to leave it, and we were both at an age when hazards and dangers have no attraction, and ambition has resolved itself into a desire for repose. But our children were young, their life was just beginning, and I did not think it right to deprive them of the advantages which civilization and contact with the world presented; and then again, Emily, since she had heard that her father was in England, naturally wanted to go to him. So at last I decided to call everyone together, and when they came I spoke to them of civilized Europe, and I asked them if they wanted to go with Captain Littelton, or would be content to pass the remainder of their lives upon this coast.

Jack and Ernest declared that they would rather stay. Ernest, the philosopher, had no need of the world, and Jack, the hunter, found the domain of Falcon's Nest large enough for his excursions. Fritz was silent, but I saw by his face that he had decided to go, so I asked him to say candidly. He confessed that he had a great desire to return to Europe, and Francis declared that he would willingly go too.

At last, then, we were to be separated; two of our sons were about to leave us, and perhaps we should never again see them. Elizabeth submitted to the sad necessity; she had a mother's objections, but she studied the advantage of her sons.

138

Mr. Wolston was also separating from one of his daughters, who was going on to New Holland. All this was very painful, and when we had made up our minds, I hastened to tell Captain Littelton. He readily consented to take three passengers.

'I am leaving three,' he said, 'Mr. and Mrs. Wolston and one of their daughters; so if I take three more, it comes to the same thing.'

The *Unicorn* remained eight days at anchor, and we employed them in preparing the cargo which was to be the fortune of our boys on arriving in Europe. All the riches that we had amassed — pearls, ivory, spices, furs, and all our rare productions — were carefully packed and put on board the ship, which we also furnished with meat and fruits.

On the eve of their departure I gave Fritz this journal of our residence on the island, and told him to have it published as soon after his arrival as he possibly could.

We none of us slept much during the last night. At the dawn of day the cannon of the ship announced the order to go on board. We went down to the shore with our sons; there they received our last kissings and blessings.

The anchor has been weighed, and the flag run up to the masthead.

I win not attempt to paint the grief of my dear Elizabeth — it is the grief of a mother, silent and profound. Jack and Ernest are trying hard to pretend they are not crying, though their eyes are full of tears, and my own grief and heartfelt sorrow is, I must confess, but badly concealed.

I finish these few lines whilst the ship's boat is waiting. My sons will thus receive my last blessing. May God ever be with them. Adieu !

THE END